Praise for *The P...*

'It had me purring with pleasure'

Daily Telegraph

'An entertaining read, moving at a clip towards a pleasingly unpredictable conclusion. . . there are some fine ideas, a rich sense of unfolding history and some nicely judged moments of philosophical whimsy and dry wit... amusing'

Time Out (London)

'A smooth translation . . . exciting'

Times Literary Supplement

'Luminous . . . a tightly spun thriller. . . . Mr. De Santis effortlessly incorporates important historical events—the building of the tower and the World's Fair—into his narrative, as well as capturing the turn-of-the-century uneasiness over the emergence of the machine age'

Wall Street Journal

'A beguiling historical whodunit'

New York Times Book Review

'Entertaining . . . Musings on the art of detecting provide many of the book's most memorable passages'

Time Out (New York)

'Discriminating general readers as well as whodunit fans will enjoy this outstanding puzzler, winner of the first Casa de América de Narrativa Prize for Best Latin American Novel . . . De Santis adroitly explores such issues as the difference between image and reality while providing intelligent and entertaining discussions of alternate approaches to detection'

Publishers Weekly (starred review)

'A complex whodunit that provokes thought as well as entertainment, on subjects from waterproof shoeshine cream to ancient Greek physics. It fires multiple, intense bursts of crime stories at the reader, some only a page or so long. And it climaxes with serial murders that tie into the building of the Eiffel Tower and the Paris World's Fair of 1889'

Associated Press

'Against the backdrop of the 1889 World's Fair, detective's assistant Sigmundo Salvatrio travels to Paris in his master's stead for a mysterious (natch) gathering of a collective known as the Twelve Detectives. Murder and mayhem ensue . . . Colourful characters and cases create a hazy atmosphere of intelligent escapism. The real subject of the book is the mysterious, melancholic birth of modernity'

Washington Post

PABLO DE SANTIS

Pablo De Santis was born in Buenos Aires, studied literature at the Universidad de Buenos Aires, and subsequently worked as a journalist and comic-strip creator, becoming editor in chief of one of Argentina's leading comic magazines. De Santis won the inaugural Premio Planeta–Casa de América de Narrativa Prize for Best Latin American Novel for *The Paris Enigma*.

Also by Pablo De Santis

The Paris Enigma

PABLO DE SANTIS

Voltaire's Calligrapher

*Translated from the Spanish
by Lisa Carter*

HARPER

Harper
An imprint of HarperCollins*Publishers*
77–85 Fulham Palace Road,
Hammersmith, London W6 8JB

www.harpercollins.co.uk

A Paperback Original 2010
1

First published in Great Britain by HarperCollins*Publishers* 2010

A catalogue record for this book is available from the British Library

ISBN: 978-0-00-726905-1

Set in Janson Text with Voluta Scripit display

Printed and bound in Great Britain by Clays Ltd, St Ives plc

 Mixed Sources

Product group from well-managed
forests and other controlled sources
www.fsc.org   Cert no. SW-COC-1806
© 1996 Forest Stewardship Council

FSC is a non-profit international organization established
to promote the responsible management of the world's forests.
Products carrying the FSC label are independently certified
to assure consumers that they come from forests that are managed
to meet the social, economic and ecological needs
of present and future generations.

Find out more about HarperCollins and the environment at
www.harpercollins.co.uk/green

Contents

PART ONE

The Hanged Man

The Relic	13
First Letters	18
Ferney	24
The Correspondence	32
The Passenger	38
Toulouse	43
The Scene of the Crime	47
The Mechanical Hand	52
The Performance	58
The Exam	63
The Bronze Bell	70
The Execution	75

PART TWO
The Bishop

The Abbot's Hand	81
A Friend of V.	88
Siccard House	95
Von Knepper's Trail	100
The Bishop's Silence	106
Kolm's Walking Stick	111
Clarissa	116
The Prisoner	120
The Burial Chamber	126
Taps on the Window	132
Fabres' Disciple	136
Mathilde's Foot	142
Flight	148
The End of the Trip	152

PART THREE

The Master Calligrapher

The Wait   157

Anonymous Libel   164

The Human Machine   172

The Halifax Gibbet   179

The Life of Statues   186

A Blank Page   193

Hammer and Chisel   197

The Locked Door   203

Silas Darel   208

Hieroglyphic   212

Inventory   216

The Marble Head   220

PART ONE

The Hanged Man

The Relic

I arrived in this port with very few belongings: four shirts, my calligraphy implements, and a heart in a glass jar. The shirts were threadbare and ink-stained, my quills ruined by the sea air. The heart, however, was intact, indifferent to the voyage, the storms, the humidity. Hearts only wear out in life; after that, nothing can hurt them.

There are countless philosophical relics in Europe today, most as fake as the bones that churches revere. Saints used to be the only protagonists of such superstition, but who today would fight over a rib, a finger, or the heart of a saint? The bones and skulls of philosophers, on the other hand, are worth a fortune.

If an unwary collector even mentions the name Voltaire to any antiquarian in Paris, he will be led to a room at the back and, in absolute secrecy, shown a heart that resembles a stone, locked in a gold cage or inside a marble urn. He will be asked to pay a fortune for it, in the name of philosophy. A hollow, funereal grandeur surrounds these fake hearts while the real one is here, on my desk, as I write. The only opulence I can offer it is the afternoon light.

I live in a cramped room, where the walls erode a little more each day. The floorboards are loose and some can be lifted with ease. That's where I hide the glass jar, when I go to work in the morning, wrapped in a frayed, red velvet cloth.

I came to this port fleeing all those who saw our profession as a reminder of the former establishment. You had to shout to be heard at the National Convention, but we calligraphers had only ever learned to defend ourselves in writing. Although someone proposed that our right hands be cut off, the egalitarian solution prevailed, and that limited itself to cutting off heads.

My colleagues never lifted their eyes from their work or tried to decipher the shouts that could be heard in the distance. They continued to patiently transcribe texts that had been assigned by now decapitated officials. Sometimes, as a warning or a threat, a smudged list of the condemned would be slipped under their doors, and they would copy it out, never noticing their own name hidden among the others.

I was able to escape because time had taught to me to look up from the page. I gave myself a new name and a new profession, and forged documents to present at the checkpoints between one district and another, one city and another. I fled to Spain, but my fugitive impulse was such that I didn't stop there; I wanted to get even farther away. With my lack of funds and ragged appearance, I boarded the only ship that offered me passage. It was the first time I had ever been on a boat, perhaps because of the memory of my parents, who had died in a shipwreck. As partial payment for my fare, I took dictation for the captain (he had a mountain of correspondence to attend to from women and creditors). Writing those letters and having my mistakes corrected was how I learned Spanish.

It was a long journey. The ship put in at port after port, but none of them seemed right. I would stare at the buildings along the coast, waiting for a sign that I had found my place, but there was only one sign I was prepared to understand: the one that says there is nowhere further to go. This was the ship's last stop.

This is a city people come to by mistake, those who are fleeing some peril or government, and wind up running away from the world. On the boat to shore, I was sure my professional life was over, that I would never see another drop of ink. Who in these dark, muddy streets could possibly need a calligrapher? I was wrong: I soon discovered a profound reverence for the written word, even greater here than in the cities of Europe. They love their signed, sealed directives; their papers that pass from hand to hand, generating still more paper; their detailed orders from Europe; their lists of items ruined during the voyage. Everything is stamped and signed with a flourish, then duly filed in a cabinet never to be seen again, swallowed up by the disarray.

Each morning, in a frigid office at city hall, I transcribe official documents and legal rulings. My colleagues often mention the name Voltaire, but they'd never believe I once worked for him. They all assume everything that arrives on these shores is either untrue or unimportant.

The Relic

A wind blows in through my window and sets everything aflutter. I place the heart on my papers to keep them from blowing away.

First Letters

When the *Retz* sank and my parents were lost, I was left in the care of my uncle, maréchal Dalessius. He asked me what my talents were, and I showed him some alphabets I had invented. On one page the letters were the branches of a tree, hinting at leaves and thorns; on another they were oriental palaces and buildings; and on the third – the most complicated – the letters were resigned to simply being letters. My uncle had been waiting for some indication of how best to get rid of me, and those sheets of paper were his answer. He sent me to Monsieur Vidors' School of Calligraphy, where the mysterious Silas Darel had studied.

My difficulties with authority soon began: I wasn't satisfied with writing alone; I wanted to invent pens and inks, to reestablish our craft. Calligraphy was a dying art, condemned by a shortage of masters, besieged by the printing press, reduced to the lone squad or man. I would scour the history books for heroes who might be considered calligraphers, but there were only heroes who never wrote a word.

The most enterprising of us, those who hoped to follow in Silas Darel's footsteps, would read whatever we could, from old school textbooks to anonymous dissertations on cryptography. Our profession was so dead that we felt like archaeologists of our own kind.

Complete silence reigned in the classroom, interrupted only by the scratching of quills on paper – a noise that was itself a metaphor for silence. The long hall had floor-to-ceiling windows on both sides, and our teachers insisted they remain open, even in winter, claiming that a well-ventilated room was essential to good penmanship. In blew dirt, twigs, and pine needles that my classmates would angrily brush off the page, but I would leave them, believing you must respect the marks of circumstance when writing. All but a few resigned themselves to using the school's supplies, purchased twice a year from a Portuguese sailor: black ink that soon lost its color, red ink full of lumps, sheets of paper whose imperfections caused letters to jump off the page as if skipping rope, and goose quill pens chosen at random.

After dinner and prayers, I would hide in my room or the garden, beside a stone fountain with green water so putrid you could write with it, and experiment with my own inventions. My favorite ink consisted of pig's blood, alcohol, and iron oxide. I would buy the left wings of black geese at the market and pluck the feathers one by one, discarding fourteen out of every fifteen. Having selected the best, I would heat sand in a copper bowl then pour it into a wooden case: there I would leave the quills to harden. I kept all of my implements in a sewing box that had belonged to my mother, and still held a bronze thimble and the smell of lavender.

When I left Vidors' School, my uncle found me a job with the courts. It was a natural fit for those of us who graduated; others wound up as librarians or as private scribes for the most distinguished families. I began to carry the tools of my trade from one government office or courthouse to another. This was an era of all things fragile and futile: I have never seen anything like it since. I was once given a death sentence to prepare, that was then shown to the convict, full of arabesques and wax seals, on his way to the gallows. He said: Thank the calligrapher for having turned my crimes into something so beautiful; I would kill ten more men just to have him create something similar again. Never, in my life, have I received higher praise.

Bottles of squid ink, scorpion venom, sulfur solution, oak leaves, and lizard heads all sat together in my room. I had also experimented with invisible inks, based on instructions I found in a copy of *De Occulta Caligraphia* that I bought from a bookseller on rue Admont, and was forbidden at Vidors' School. It promised water-based inks that would become visible upon contact with blood, or when rubbed with snow, or exposed for long hours to the light of a cloudless moon. Other inks took the opposite route, and would go from black to gray and then disappear altogether.

My career in the courts came to an end when I prepared the death sentence for Catherine de Béza, convicted of murdering her husband, General de Béza. When the general fell ill, his wife sent for his long-time physician –

a man who, nearly blind, was prone to prescribing obsolete medications and signing death certificates with no questions asked. But that very morning the old doctor awoke with a fever and sent his young protégé instead. By the time he arrived, the general was already dead. It took no more than a minute for the young physician to determine it wasn't of natural causes: he peered under the cadaver's nails with a magnifying glass and found traces of arsenic.

Madame de Béza was tried and found guilty. She was taken to the gallows, but the executioner was unable to proceed: the page containing the verdict, covered in writing just a few hours earlier, was now a blank sheet enlivened only by red wax seals. Some understood the disappearance to be a sign from God, attributing it to the virtue of the accused rather than the folly of the calligrapher, and so Catherine's noose was exchanged for jail.

As for me, they tried to accuse me of conspiracy; I attempted to explain my mistake using arguments of science and fate but was still sent to prison for three months.

I went to my uncle's as soon as I was released, yearning to sleep night and day in a real bed, free of the stench, the screams, and the rats. My uncle, however, had already gathered my things, and his cold embrace celebrated not my return but my departure.

'I took the liberty of offering your services while you were in prison. I sent some old acquaintances a brief list of your abilities and a long list of your incompetence, so as not to be called a liar.'

'Did anyone respond?'

'The only reply came from Château Ferney. They read everything backwards there: they understood your vices as virtues, and agreed to hire you immediately.'

Ferney

I was twenty years old and all I owned was a sewing box full of quills and inks. It would have been impossible to get to Ferney if my uncle, maréchal Dalessius, hadn't run a company called Night Mail that transported the fallen. Hundreds of bodies arrived in France during wartime that had to be returned to their cities and towns. The post had initially seen to this, but letters and merchandise would arrive in such a deplorable state that people stopped reading their correspondence; as soon as the mail arrived, it was burned. The dead had managed to isolate the outer regions of our kingdom.

The Night Mail was devoted solely to funeral transport. My uncle inherited the business from my grandfather, and operations were run out of a warehouse on the outskirts of Paris that had once been a meat salting facility. There the bodies were sorted, put into coffins – often filled with salt, as if to maintain the tradition – and sent out on the roadways of France. There were only twenty-five hearses; since routes were uncertain and mistakes common, families could wait months for a body to arrive. At first, in the clamor of war, the fallen were received as heroes, but as time wore on and the fighting came to an end, the traveler would reach home like a postman bearing bad news, an inopportune visitor who spoke of a conflict everyone had managed to forget.

My uncle had a small shuttered window put in the caskets, to view the occupant and thus prevent mistakes. Another of his innovations was to hire a button manufacturer to strike medals so every soldier could be given a set. In this way, everyone went home a hero. We have very strict rules in this profession, maréchal Dalessius would say: Wear black, work at night, keep silent.

Business would fall dramatically whenever there were no wars or epidemics. In order to build up his clientele, my uncle began to disseminate a Benedictine theologian's theory: he asserted that, to get into heaven, a person must be buried in his birthplace, or at a distance of no more than that between Bethlehem and the Holy Sepulcher. This little ruse, plus an agreement with the government to cart corpses from the gallows and prisons, ensured my uncle was never short of patrons, even in the worst times of peace.

Ferney was far away, on the Swiss border. Banished from Paris by the king, Voltaire had bought the château to be able to escape to his estate in Geneva if his life were ever in danger. By the time we arrived, all of the bodies had been delivered and I was the only remaining passenger. I said good-bye to Servin, the coachman, and stood alone at the door to the castle.

A clerk studied my papers then told me to take a seat. The sun soon faded from the windows, and I was left in the dark. No one came to light the lamps; I thought I had been forgotten. It had been an exhausting trip. All I wanted was food and a bed, but a servant finally appeared and led me to the east wing of the castle. There were clocks in every room and the noise was deafening. This tick-tock, I soon learned, was so pervasive it crept into the domestic staff's dreams, tormenting them with images of gears, hands, and Roman numerals.

Voltaire had seen his share of conflict, prison, and exile; I expected to see a giant of a man, with an enormous head and piercing eyes. Instead I found an old man who seemed unreal, more like a drawing in a book (a book left in the garden through a night of rain). His teeth had been lost to scurvy, his bald head was covered in a woolen cap, and his tongue, thanks to his habit of licking his quill whenever it ran dry, was as blue as a hanged man's.

Voltaire didn't turn when I walked into the room; perhaps he was deaf as well. He was studying a sheaf of papers with a gold-rimmed magnifying glass.

'Idiot,' he said.

'Sorry I'm late.'

'The man who wrote this is an idiot.'

'One of your enemies?'

'Worse: me. Why this stupid fondness for dictionaries? Can you tell me that? It must have rubbed off when I worked on the *Encylopédie*.'

'As a calligrapher, I'm quite fond of alphabetical order, too.'

I recalled how this had been taken to such an extreme at Vidors' School that we would use our bodies to form letters in gymnasium class. *G* and *h* were the worst. Out in the bitterly cold patio, our teacher would stand in a tower and recite passages from the *Aenid* in Latin that we were forced to spell out all morning long.

'Do you know, I once planned to write my autobiography using alphabetical order. If I ever undertake such a venture, remember that any letter can be omitted except *a* and *z*. They give the impression of having come full circle, even if other letters are missing in the middle. Who knows what Christianity might have become if Jesus had said "I am Beta and Psi" instead of "I am Alpha and Omega."'

He handed me a pen and paper.

'Show me a sample of your calligraphy.'

'I'd rather use my own quills, if you don't mind.'

'It was thanks to them that you lost your last job. Who's to say you won't lose the next?'

I refused to be intimidated.

'What should I write?'

'"My hand trembles like an old man's."'

Indeed, my hand did tremble. The result was wretched-looking. This had never happened to me before.

'It's the pen.'

'Try another.'

I took out a blue goose quill, my favorite, and the result was even worse.

'That goose is still flapping its wings. Still, I'll hire you. Your hand shakes so badly people will think I've written it myself. You'll report to my secretary, Wagnière.'

'And what will I do?'

'Answer correspondence. Here, in this room. You'll need to consult me regarding some replies. Others will be at your discretion.'

'But it will be obvious you didn't write them.'

'Don't worry. In fact, it's better that way. People will think: If he's not drafting his own letters, he must be hard at work on an important play. Absence itself can be an element of style.'

We were suddenly startled by a crashing sound. Voltaire headed into the hallway, and I followed. His strides were long but slow, and I had to stop myself from racing ahead. Though it took us a while to get there, papers were still floating in the air, as if waiting for their owner to arrive.

We entered the archives at the same time as a tall man

with a sad air about him, dressed in somber clothing. He began to dig among the piles, and I knelt down to help. Someone was coughing and moaning under the weight of those yellowing letters tied with string.

I pulled out a bundle of moth-eaten pages that nearly disintegrated in my hands. Down below was a face so covered in dust it seemed to form part of the correspondence.

'Let's get poor Barras out of here. You take one arm and I'll take the other.'

We pulled out a weedy young man whose head and upper lip were bleeding. He shook us off at the first opportunity, as anxious to leave as if a wild beast were laying in wait for him. He limped down the hallway, shouting:

'I'm going back to the kitchen! To the archives, never again!'

'I think we need a new file clerk,' the tall man said to Voltaire.

'Here he is. Wagnière, let me introduce you to Dalessius. Dalessius, straighten up this mess. In addition to writing letters, from now on you'll be in charge of the archives.'

'Isn't it dangerous for an apprentice?' Wagnière asked. 'Barras nearly died and last month, that student from Alsace. . .'

'If M. Dalessius tries, he'll learn. If not, he'll be sent home. . . in the same carriage that brought him here.'

The Correspondence

Voltaire had many enemies, so opening his mail was a dangerous task. There could be poisonous needles concealed between the pages, vials that emitted toxic fumes, venomous spiders.

The packages he received were often hollow books that contained hibernating snakes or sensitive incendiary devices. In a special room, away from the rest so as to limit the number of victims, I would check every envelope and parcel with a paralyzed heart. To assist in the task, Voltaire had bought a series of instruments in Geneva designed to detect tricks and explosives: rock-crystal magnifying glasses, a fine telescope that could be inserted through packaging, a lamp with a blue flame that allowed you to see through paper.

I not only opened the correspondence, but I also replied to it, in Voltaire's name.

'Look in my books and add some old witticism to your seminarian's prose,' he ordered.

I was young, and that work – which I would later miss dearly – filled me with impatience. The routine, even the danger, bored me: I began to open the mail without looking and reply without thinking. To my surprise, Voltaire received letters from a number of amorous women, written in their own blood. If they could only have seen the living corpse that was the object of such futile passion, they'd have scraped it all up to put back in their veins. Out of sheer tedium, I began to answer my employer's correspondence using all of the implements at my disposal. There was nothing I wouldn't use: albatross quills hardened in the iodine from sea foam; Chinese monkey hair brushes; inks that shone in the dark; others that disappeared as you read the words, creating the illusion of good-bye. Initially enthused by my own enthusiasm, Voltaire soon grew annoyed that his letters would be blank by the time they reached their destination, or contain jumbled words, or a signature that glowed like a ghost in the night.

To limit my experiments, Wagnière reminded me I still had to organize the archives. There were so many bundles of letters that if you took all the yellow and red ribbons that held them together, you could tie a bow around the world. Correspondence from royalty, like Catherine the Great or the King of Prussia, was to be kept in an iron chest, under lock and key. Insulting letters were burned, like the ones from the Bishop of Annecy, who every fortnight would accuse Voltaire of unconfessed sins. The ridiculous ones were burned as well, like those from a society of alchemists in Geneva that swore they possessed Paracelsus himself. *We keep him hidden in the cellar, in a house on the lakeshore. He awakes every three months, mumbles something that sounds like Voltaire, and returns to his centuries-long sleep.*

I had never had any trouble with the little iron stove until one day (I was distracted, reading some licentious notes from Mme. F.) a spark set fire to a pile of correspondence from the marquis d'Argenson, a dear friend of Voltaire's. I always carried a bag of sand for making quills and sometimes to use as a blotting agent, and threw it on the fire before it burned the archives to the ground.

I couldn't sleep that night, knowing Voltaire would be deciding my fate: expulsion or servitude.

I went to his study at dawn. Through the window, a stand of dark trees mirrored my sadness, the wind bending them into question marks. Voltaire was examining a parasite he had found on one of his plants.

'We must get rid of everything that consumes us, everything that lives at the expense of others,' Voltaire said by way of greeting. 'I want you to pack your bags.'

'Can't you give me some other job, instead of sending me away? Don't you need a gardener?'

'What do you know about plants? Whenever you go into the garden, the roses impale themselves on their own thorns and the tulips commit mass suicide.'

'What about the kitchen?'

'They would cook you, and I'm not sure I'd like that dish.'

I liked life at Ferney. I didn't want to go back to climbing stairs at the courts, knocking on magistrates' doors, waiting in paper-filled offices where the air was always stale. All the strength drained out of me as I thought about leaving, and while Voltaire stood tall in front of me, I grew old and stooped.

'I'll go pack now and never return,' I said, feigning dignity and hoping for compassion.

'What did you think I meant? I'm not firing you. I need you to get ready to leave, but to go to Toulouse.'

'Why Toulouse?'

'A traveler arrived last night and told me of a distressing case. He said the court of Languedoc is preparing to execute a Protestant named Jean Calas, and perhaps all of his family as well.'

'What is he accused of?'

'Of killing his son.'

'Then I hope the sentence is carried out.'

'And I hope you'll find out why they're determined to kill this man at all costs. I've prepared some briefs; you can read them on the way.'

'But I'm a calligrapher. I care about the clarity of line, not the truth behind words. That's for others to do; philosophers, for example.'

'I'm too old to go. Besides, my reputation there guarantees it's a shortcut to death. I'm in no hurry to die, much less in Toulouse. You, on the other hand, won't be in any danger, as long as you never mention my name. I've already asked your uncle to send a coach for you.'

'I thought I'd stay here, to write for you and for history, not travel with the dead.'

'If your path is one of history, then it's only natural to be accompanied by the dead.'

The Passenger

The old coachman, Servin, came from the Swiss side of the border this time. He was transporting a couple from Avignon who had been killed in an avalanche. The tragedy had occurred ten years earlier, but the bodies had only recently been found. They were accompanied by a third coffin, but I didn't bother to ask about it.

Three hours into our trip it began to rain. Ahead were only shadows and darkened trees. I shouted to see whether Servin wanted me to take a turn, but he didn't reply; he took another swig from his bottle and spurred on the horses, indifferent to the storm.

He soon told me to get some sleep so I could take over

for him later. A small iron cot hung down inside the carriage above the three coffins. I crawled up into it, settled onto one blanket, and pulled another one over me. I fell asleep for a few minutes, despite the swaying bed and squeaking chains, but a sudden jolt woke me from a dream in which I was supposed to take Voltaire's body to some faraway place. Seconds later a violent lurch tossed me into the air and onto the third coffin.

The shuttered viewing window snapped open, as if someone had answered my knock. I peered in at the third passenger with the help of intermittent lightning bolts. It was the same curiosity that had led me, as a boy, to stare at the hanged man's blue tongue, the soles of his feet carved with unrecognizable symbols, and the superstitious old women patiently pulling his nails and teeth. I could already picture the unsightly powdered face when I saw her: she had been beautiful, and that hadn't changed. Her features spoke not of death, but enchantment. I had found a secret door into a fairy tale.

I shouted for Servin to stop and waited for the storm to bring us another flash of lightning. The coachman didn't bat an eye.

'Sometimes a dry climate preserves a body intact.'

'You call this rain a dry climate?'

'Maybe they embalmed her the Egyptian way. They say there are funeral parlors in Geneva that cover a body in animal fat and replace the organs with sawdust.'

I wanted him to stay and discuss the enigma, but he went back to the reins, unburdened by the curiosity that leads one to search for answers and find only problems.

We hid the carriage behind a copse of trees and spent the night in an inn, keeping the nature of our cargo from the owner or she would never have let us stay: gravediggers, Night Mail coachmen, and executioners were generally unwelcome guests. It was still raining outside and there was a leak above my bed. I moved, but the drips followed me, reminding me there was still a mystery to be solved.

I lowered myself out through a window, being careful not to wake Servin. Inside the hearse, I used the lamp I had brought to illuminate the face behind the glass. The closer I brought the light, the darker it was all around. The woman's lips were pursed, as if she were about to reveal a secret. No Egyptian technique was capable of such perfection.

The next morning Servin found me asleep on top of the coffin and woke me with a cuff on the head.

'I'm going to tell the Maréchal. That's all he needs, for you to fall in love with a passenger. You take the horses as far as Avignon.'

I let the horses take me. They seemed much wiser, their soft side-to-side motion indicating a philosophical acceptance of the world's contradictions. I began to talk to them and was sure they understood by the way they would sometimes toss their heads, as if agreeing with my arguments.

The storm had ended by the time Servin took the reins again. I didn't dare tell him I was lost, but one glance at the surrounding forest and the old coachman immediately turned the horses around. He found the road to Avignon, delivered the two bodies from the Alps, and pocketed an enormous tip. He gave me less than a tenth, but promised I would earn a little more once we reached Toulouse.

Whenever we passed through a town to replenish our food supplies, residents would close their windows and cross their fingers: the passing of a Night Mail coach was a bad omen. Twice we were refused entrance and forced to go another way. I tried to convince Servin to remove the black crêpe and carved allegorical images that decorated the hearse. Without these, it would look like any other carriage, but he refused.

'Maréchal Dalessius personally decorates each coach and no changes are allowed. He wants us to be recognized from afar. Alternate routes and delays shouldn't concern us. As he says: A detour is just another road.'

Toulouse

I had been eager to arrive but now that the wheels (about to take one last turn before falling off their axles) were shakily tracing the route to Toulouse, I felt that mixture of exhaustion and unease that comes over a traveler whenever he reaches a new city.

We delivered the last coffin to the rue des Aveugles. The house belonged to M. Girard, a toy manufacturer. A long table displayed wooden horses painted blue, puzzles of city maps, porcelain dolls, and armies of tin soldiers that seemed to be returning in defeat: broken, hungry, their flag in tatters.

'Is she your daughter?' I asked.

'The Night Mail is known for not asking questions,' Girard replied.

'That's true, sir,' Servin said, worried my curiosity might reduce or eliminate the tip altogether. 'Please forgive him. Young Dalessius is new to the profession.'

The owner gave us each a few coins, but Servin snatched mine from me.

'You should be glad you rode here for free,' he said under his breath.

He asked the toy manufacturer whether he wanted us to move the coffin to another room in the house.

'Just there is fine,' Girard said, anxious for us to leave. Since we were no longer in danger of losing the tip, I asked about the cause of death.

'She ate a poison apple,' he snapped, pushing us toward the door.

We came out of the house, and Servin said good-bye there and then. A shipment was waiting for him on the outskirts of the city. He offered his hand, and in it was a coin. He told me to take care, and if anyone asked who sent me, to say anything at all, that I was an emissary to the devil or the Huguenots themselves, but under no circumstances was I to tell the truth.

I found lodgings near the market and took a room where I had to pay two nights in advance.

'Are you here for the festivities?' the proprietor asked. His face was scarred by illness and injury, and he was missing three fingers on his right hand.

'No. Is something happening tonight?'

'Celebrations begin in a few days.'

'And what are you celebrating?'

'The day the people of Toulouse had the courage to get rid of four thousand Huguenots. It's the two hundredth anniversary.'

'They were expelled?'

'Straight to the hereafter. Never, sir, will you see such fireworks – not even in China! I lost three fingers when I was igniting them fifteen years ago, but don't think I regret it. The moment I was hurt, I thought: Others have to smell gunpowder and are blown to pieces on the battlefield; I get to be a hero right here. I'd do it again, especially now, with the Calas family as the guests of honor. A whole year of boredom, sitting by the fire, greeting visitors as they come and go; a whole year of waiting just to watch the world explode. I can start to feel my lost fingers as the day draws closer.'

That night I looked out the window in my room and saw five men dressed in white robes, hoods pulled up, carrying an image of Christ. Voltaire had warned me: Be careful of the White Penitents. Windows opened as they passed and wilted flowers showered down on their linen hoods.

The Scene of the Crime

The room I took was cramped and cold. Previous guests had scratched their names into the musty walls. The blanket was so dirty it was much heavier and warmer than if it had been clean. Insects of every kind crawled along the floor. As I waited for sleep to free me from these annoyances, I studied the bugs with my magnifying glass. I even kept a few specimens: I liked to press them between the pages of my books as reminders.

The next morning, I bought a fresh loaf of bread. The bakers of Toulouse were paying homage to the Calas boy: it was in the shape of a hanged man, sprinkled with salt and raisins, the little noose decorated with sesame seeds.

I finished reading Voltaire's briefs and set out for the Calas house.

The judges had ordered a twenty-four hour guard be posted there. I asked the only soldier on duty if I was allowed to go in, but he said no. I had predicted as much and pulled out a bottle of wine with a loaf of that bread. The guard stepped aside, and I wandered through the now empty rooms.

All of the inhabitants had been hauled away: the father, the mother, the sister, the brother, the friend who was visiting, even the maid was in prison, and every last piece of furniture had disappeared as well. All that remained was the large, rusty nail that had held Marc-Antoine's rope. I felt I had crossed all of France just to see that nail.

'Why didn't anyone take it?' I asked the soldier.

'They say it's cursed. No one wants to touch it.'

I walked over to test its strength and show him I wasn't superstitious, but changed my mind.

'Were you here when they looted the house?'

'No, but I was told they came down the street singing and carrying torches. As soon as they got here, they stopped and stood in silence: inspiration had vanished and they didn't know what to do, whether to kneel down or lay waste. Their enthusiasm was renewed the moment they stepped through the door: most of them had never been in a house like this, and they discovered what fun it was to empty drawers and upend furniture. Other people's lives are such mysteries. At some point, one of the women wanted to burn down the house and set fire to a curtain; the others put it out and nearly set her on fire. They all arrived together but left alone, arrived singing but left in silence, arrived with torches but disappeared in darkness.'

I studied every last corner with my magnifying glass as the guard followed me around. There were fewer signs of the Calas family's whole life than of the looters' brief stay: tatters of clothing, splinters of wood, chicken bones, and broken bottles.

'There aren't enough saints in these godless times; that's why people are willing to pay such a high price for relics. You can buy the hanged man's teeth on the black market for two francs apiece.'

'I wonder if they're even real.'

'Oh, the hundreds of teeth, nails, and locks of hair for sale are all real. By the time I came on duty, only the martyr's books were left. No one wanted them because books aren't relics. But you seem like you might be interested. Maybe we could come to an arrangement.'

The guard mentioned an exorbitant sum. I gave no reply but concentrated on examining the nail instead. He dropped the price lower and lower until, discouraged and irritated, he knew he had no choice but to listen to my offer.

'I'll tell you what,' I proposed as I cleaned the magnifying glass on my shirt. 'I don't have the money to buy the books, but if you let me look at them I'll pay you one coin now and another when I'm done.'

He agreed and went to the window to make sure no one was coming.

'I've hidden them.'

We went into what had been the maid's room. The soldier lifted up some floorboards and handed me five dusty books. I surreptitiously looked for even a scrap of paper that might have been left behind, but all I found were notes penciled in the margins beside certain passages. I read the titles of the works: a collection of essays by Seneca, organized by topic; *Hamlet* by William Shakespeare; a speech by Cicero; *The Apology of Socrates* by Plato; and a fifth book that, no matter how hard I try, refuses to come to mind. Every paragraph the reader had marked praised death at one's own hand. He hadn't been so distraught or depressed that he committed suicide; he had prepared himself until he was ready for the rope.

'These could save the Calas family. Why don't you take them to the court?'

'Books have never saved anyone. It's too late for them anyhow. We need a martyr: the fanatics need one and so do we, men like you and me who don't know what to believe in. My mother had a boil on her left leg that was already affecting her knee; she went to the funeral, prayed, and it went away. How do you explain that? Pray to the hanged man!'

'I'd rather pray to a saint with a little more experience.'

'Well, I've been blessed by him: I've already earned one coin and now I'm about to earn another.'

He held out his hand. I paid and left the ransacked house.

The Mechanical Hand

All around the Church of St. Stephen, relic vendors secretly displayed their little trophies in glass jars so thick they deformed and enlarged the treasures inside. The church was full of parishioners who needed increasing amounts of incense, which created an impregnating fog. The candles cast their yellow hue on the darkness. A blackened skeleton hung down, a tag proclaiming it was property of the Toulouse school of medicine. In its right hand was a quill dipped in blood and in its left a palm leaf, symbols of the conversion the murder had prevented. Used to being a simple object of study, the skeleton seemed taken aback by such sanctification.

I walked on to the courthouse where the Calas family was being tried. Armed guards stood at the door, and no one was allowed to enter. Conversations continued inside even though it was late; the windows above were illuminated. About a hundred people were gathered outside, circulating rumors and looking up as if the wavering light might contain a message. Everyone who came in or out of the court was accosted for news; though none replied, the crowd saw its hopes and convictions confirmed by the hush. The only person not questioned was a tall man in a cloak, who seemed to impose silence from afar and whose every step was like a period at the end of an empty phrase. I heard a whisper beside me:

'That one there cleaned the body. He used to be an executioner.'

I followed the man in the cloak, rummaging in my bag for coins to pay for any information he could provide. He strode along briskly, and I had to run to keep pace. Windows closed and lights went out as we passed, giving the distinct impression his steps had ordered them to. I stopped next to a fountain whose waters were black: my quarry had disappeared. Before I knew it, I felt a rope around my neck and my feet were off the ground, not very high but enough that I longed to feel the earth below. The moon was reflected on the water. I struggled in vain, dancing the final jig of the hanged.

'The last man who tried to rob me lost his right hand. I carry it in a box of salt; it brings me luck wherever I go.'

I tried to speak but couldn't. I reached into my pocket for a coin and let it fall on the cobblestones. My attacker dismantled the gallows, and my feet touched down once more.

'I came to pay you, not rob you,' I said.

'I'm not selling anything.'

'I buy words.'

'I don't talk much.'

'I heard you washed the body of Marc-Antoine Calas.'

He wanted to know what so interested me that I was willing to pay for answers. I told him I worked for the Jesuits, and that they wanted to be absolutely certain the Calas boy was a martyr. The Jesuits, I explained, were trying to speed up the canonization process for priests who had been murdered in the Orient, and didn't want any old impromptu veneration to supersede the urgent needs of the Church. I handed him another silver coin.

The executioner spoke:

'I attended to the body until the White Penitents took it from me. Six of them came down to the courthouse basement, showed me a piece of paper I never got to read, and carried it out in procession.'

'Was he bruised, as if hanged by force?'

'Not a single mark, other than a scar on his left shoulder – a very old wound.'

We sat on the edge of the fountain.

'I wasn't going to kill you. It's bad luck to kill a man on a full moon: he'll haunt your dreams.'

The executioner had big hands scarred by ropes and blades. I told him I knew about his former profession.

'I've beheaded criminals in Paris, hanged poor wretches in Marseille, and pushed offenders off the top of a tower in Italy. They would land on marble below, and a painter would capture their final pose. But the real art is the ax: not many can cut off a head with a single blow. The rope, on the other hand, is the simplest yet least reliable of all the methods.'

'Why? Did someone survive?'

'Only one man lived to say "I was executed by Kolm." He paid my assistant to fray the rope so it would break when he dropped. A man can't be hanged twice for the same crime in Marseille, so he was set free. But let's talk about happier things.'

Kolm worked for the courts in Toulouse, where he washed bodies in tubs of bleach water, sutured wounds, and sometimes determined cause of death. He was hired because of his experience as an executioner.

'Do you miss your old profession?'

'No. I got tired of being needed but despised. Take a look at this walking stick.'

He held up a long cane made of dark wood. On the bottom was a small but perfect replica of a hand, operated by a mechanism on the silver handle.

'I was never allowed to touch any food when I went to the market. No one would speak to me. Then I had an artisan from Nuremberg make this walking stick. At first no one had a problem greeting the silver hand, letting it pick up apples or fish. But then it started to malfunction and now it crushes everything it touches.'

The hand opened and closed. Kolm invited me to try it. I lifted the walking stick and, as I looked up, saw a woman standing in a window. It was the passenger we had delivered to the toy manufacturer on rue des Aveugles.

I heard the sound of the window as it closed.

I had no intention of saying anything, but suddenly heard my voice, as if it were another's:

'A dead woman just closed a window.'

'I know the dead and I know they never come back; I'd have been visited by now if they did.' Kolm looked over at the house. It was the only one that still had any lights on. A bronze bell hung out front. 'There are seventeen women who work there. They might disappear during the day, but they come back to life at night.'

His words did nothing to reassure me, and I hurried away down the deserted street. I don't know why, but Kolm followed me, and the moon followed him.

The Performance

I went to see Kolm two days later, as he had promised to ask whether there were any openings at the court for a calligrapher. Kolm lived in a rooming house reserved for the brotherhood of executioners; they owned a building in every city to avoid the usual problems of lodging. Never having executed anyone, I wasn't allowed in, but Kolm told me the rooms were decorated with axes, hoods, and belts that had belonged to legendary executioners. These made him nostalgic. I asked why he had left such a profitable profession.

'Five years ago I helped to suppress an uprising against M. Ressing. I had cut off about ten heads when it seemed a pair of familiar eyes was staring up at me. I reached into the bloody basket and found my father's head. We hadn't seen one another in a long time, and I had executed him without even noticing. I know he recognized me, and yet he didn't say a word: he wouldn't interrupt my work. I haven't executed anyone since. I was only able to recover my father's head, which I put in a glass case and took to the town where he was born. There I gave him the funeral he deserved. For his epitaph I wrote: *Theodor Kolm lies here. And elsewhere as well.*'

It was Sunday and Kolm's day off. We walked until we saw a crowd beside the market: a theatre company was performing *The Calas Murderers*.

The actors had erected a stage in a derelict square, amid statues of sleeping horses. The church had never been kind to actors, refusing for centuries to bury them in hallowed ground, but this company had chosen a topic of such popular interest that the White Penitents had even agreed to pay for the production. That night I wrote an account of the play and sent it to Ferney:

The Calas family is sitting at the table. A friend arrives from far away. He begins to talk about his city. After a while, he realizes they aren't paying attention; no one is responding to his comments. The father, Jean Calas, finally interrupts him: he says they have a decision to make.

Marc-Antoine is preparing to convert to Catholicism, the father explains. He has been shut away in his room, reading the Bible, for the past seventeen days. We've hidden spiders and snakes between the pages, but nothing distracts him.

At night, the mother says, we give him candles with most of the wick removed, so they won't last long. But he keeps reading, using mirrors to capture the moonlight. Then, on nights when there is no moon, in absolute darkness, he repeats the sacred words – words that aren't sacred to us.

Is there no way to convince him, the friend asks. Women? A trip?

We've tried everything, the father says. Now we must sacrifice the lamb.

But he's our lamb, the mother says. If we wait just a little longer...

The father says: Tomorrow he'll sign his conversion at St. Stephen's, and he can finally work as a lawyer. He may take action against us, to prove his sincerity. There is no faith more dangerous than the faith of the converted.

Where will we do it, the friend asks.

There's a nail upstairs, above the door, the father says. We never found any use for it, but it was too big to pull out.

Perhaps we should wait until tomorrow, the mother says.

The rope is impatient, the father says.

In silence, they head upstairs. Jean Calas leads the group, rope in hand.

Marc-Antoine is reading in bed when they interrupt him.

We've come to talk to you.

With a rope? That's a strange conversation.

Let's talk about the decision you're going to make.

It's too late. They're expecting me. I renounce the Lutheran faith.

Then there's no other option, the father says.

When will you do it, the son asks. I'd like to finish this paragraph about martyrdom first.

The father tears out the page and shoves the ball of paper into his son's mouth.

There's no need to read about martyrs: you'll soon know from experience.

The mother and the friend hold him. The father slides the noose over his head. The three of them lift him up and hang him.

The show was so successful that indignant spectators threw rocks at the performers, mistaking them for the people they were playing.

The head of the company, who was in the role of Jean Calas, had to shout to be heard.

'Don't vent your rage on us; we're only actors. But we so believe in this play that our Marc-Antoine is a real hanged man. A mistake sent him to the gallows in Marseille, and a miracle saved him.'

From the dais, Marc-Antoine let the public see the scars on his neck.

'I was that man's executioner,' Kolm whispered in my ear. 'He's the living image of my failure.'

'What does it matter? You're no longer in the profession.'

We left the crowd and the shouting behind.

'Once an executioner, always an executioner.'

The Exam

Kolm accompanied me to the courthouse where I would take the calligraphy exam. There were new hires every week as calligraphers left, overwhelmed by the disorganization in the courts, the contradictory orders, and the fear of poisoned ink. A legend about a cursed word circulated among the local profession: everything would be fine until that word appeared in a court document, then whoever wrote it would suffer misfortune.

I sat the exam with twenty other young men, in a long hall on wooden benches that had been carved with pen knives. You could learn better calligraphy from those furtive inscriptions than from any dissertation. I soon realized I was much slower than the others and knew I was done.

'You can go,' the examiner said. 'I don't know why you bothered to come when your hand writes at a snail's pace.'

'My hand may be slow, but it knows where it's going. Have you ever seen a snail retrace its steps to correct a mistake? Come out to the patio with me.'

When we reached the edge of a pond, I asked his name.

'Tellier.'

Using an oily ink, I wrote his name on the surface of the water, but backwards, mirrored. Then, when I brought a sheet of Japanese paper to the water, his name was imprinted the right way around, with a few walnut leaves (little more than veins) as decoration. He hired me on the spot.

I was taken to a room where I was given a blue cloak and a bronze plaque that read *Calligrapher* to hang around my neck.

And so, in the coming days, I was able to wander through the archives of Languedoc, draw up documents, and take notes on the sessions being held in the

Calas case. Everyone seemed bored of it already, as if the protagonists had died ages ago, and judges and their clerks were sadly responsible for keeping the memory of a bygone event alive. Witnesses for the defense filed through: the Calas family had never done anyone wrong, they had nothing against Catholics; their eldest son, who lived outside Toulouse, had converted, and they still sent him a monthly stipend. But they couldn't compete with the flood of miracles brought by the prosecution: the blind could see, the crippled could walk, and incurable ills would disappear when you prayed to the hanged man.

I wrote to tell Voltaire that the tragic day was drawing near, that the lawyer for the Calas family had managed to save the lives of the mother, the sister, and the brother, but the father was doomed. The most far-fetched of all possible versions had prevailed: Jean Calas, a 65-year-old man, had slipped the noose around his son's neck, overcome his resistance, and hung him from the door all on his own.

My fanaticism for calligraphy soon helped me earn the trust of my superiors. I took advantage of every opportunity to declare that the printing press (ever ready to spread the worst ideas) and the *Encylopédie* (its most recent work, an impious summary of the world) stripped words of all transcendental meaning. A calligrapher, on the other hand, brought the world closer; like the ancient scribes, he writes in order to illuminate. Tellier and his subordinates were won over by my opinions. So vehemently did I defend my art using theological arguments that I wound up believing my own fabrications. Even now, as I transcribe official documents at city hall, I sometimes still repeat the words: God made the world without a printing press, by hand, letter by letter. And that thought, or, at least the struggle to believe it, justifies all of the many hours.

One afternoon Tellier had me deliver a scroll to the Dominican monastery. I took the long way in order to pass by Bell Manor. All of the inhabitants were asleep; none of the windows were open.

A hooded monk stopped me at the monastery gate. I told him I was to deliver the documents directly to Father Razin. He looked at the bronze plaque around my neck and led me down a corridor to a set of stairs. In front of me was an ornate door, and I hesitated over whether to open it or continue downstairs. My escort had disappeared. I knocked discreetly but no one answered: the wood was so thick the sound never reached the other side. I pushed the door just wide enough to peer in.

Purple drapes accentuated the air of seclusion inside. Large torches cast bright light nearby, but it dissipated farther on, leaving the back of the room obscured. Five monks were bent over enormous maps and city plans. No one looked up at me. Their conversation consisted of whispers and hand gestures. They were studying lands crisscrossed by rivers and mountain ranges, cities divided into plots, and here and there they would place little lead pieces depicting crosses and pitchforks. It was as if they were caught up in an achingly slow game that had started years earlier, the rules having been lost somewhere along the way.

An iron hand came down on my shoulder.

'Not there,' said the monk who had let me in. 'Downstairs.'

He pushed me impatiently, and I nearly fell down the well-worn stairs.

Father Razin, head of the White Penitents, the most fanatical branch of the Dominicans, was sitting behind a desk. His claw-like hand snatched the documents from me. He read them in a wink, then scrawled a few lines on a sheet of paper.

'This wax seal had better remain intact. We've already lost three messengers to blunders or betrayal.'

It was late and the courts would be empty: I would have to deliver the message the next morning. I took the letter to my room and slipped it under my pillow. The minute I did, I heard a thunderous voice from a faraway castle order me to open it.

It was a tremendous risk, but I had worked with similar seals before. First I used molten lead to make a mold of the seal, then I broke it, peeling it off the page with a fine stiletto. Finally, a steam bath with eucalyptus leaves opened the letter.

Razin's handwriting had nearly torn the paper: 'Report to Paris regarding news in this matter. The Lord has blessed us with a rash of miracles; the name Marc-Antoine can no longer be tarnished. Our problem now is the woman Girard received from Switzerland. He is using her as an attraction at Bell Manor. No other creature of Von Knepper's is to be allowed in the Kingdom of France. I need two men you trust. I will take care of the rest. Evil uses angelic means; Good now needs diabolical means.'

I melted wax and filled the mold I had made, then replaced the seal. Once dry, I patiently filed it to eliminate any possible imperfection.

Tellier's impatience worked in my favor: he broke the seal without even looking.

'It smells of eucalyptus,' was all he said after reading the letter.

'I left early to go for a walk and got lost in the woods.'

Tellier handed me several dull-looking coins, as if blackened by smoke. These were just the key I needed to gain entrance to Bell Manor.

The Bronze Bell

A tall guard stood silently at the door, waiting for a password it took me a few seconds to guess: I showed him the money I had brought.

'Is this enough for the woman in the top window?'

He said nothing, but stepped aside to let me pass.

Five men sat in worn, red velvet armchairs waiting their turn for rooms and women. They sat in darkness, as withdrawn as monks, not a hint of lust in their postures, only boredom, shyness perhaps, a pale imitation of dignity. Each one was wearing a mask: a dog, a rabbit, a bear. During Carnival, people find pleasure in hiding their faces and showing their masks, but the men there seemed to want to hide those as well, as if the chosen animal might reveal something of their identity. I was given a bear mask and told to wait in a corner.

Every once in a while a dwarf would come into the waiting room and ring a bronze bell in the face of the chosen, then lead him away. The little bell was an exact replica of the one outside the front door and sounded muffled, as if it were under water. We all waited anxiously to hear the dwarf's footsteps; well aware of our interest, he would stomp down each oak stair.

I had started to nod off when the bell woke me, and the dwarf's white face was in front of mine. We climbed several flights of stairs to the top floor. My guide opened a leather bag and had me deposit all of the money I had brought. Then he let me in and closed the door behind me.

The first thing I saw was a folding screen, decorated with what could have been women or dragons, depending on the light. I walked around it and saw a large bed; the woman was laying in it, gold and black shell-patterned sheets pulled up to her neck. Her eyes were open and an icy cold emanated from her, filling the room. Like the figures on the screen, she could also take the shape of a woman or a dragon, depending on the whim of the light.

I said what I had come to say: the truth. It was, like all truths, a sort of good-bye.

'I don't know how you can be alive. I don't know if you have an identical twin or it's a spell or if I've lost my mind. But soon, maybe even today, the White Penitents are going to kill you. If you come with me, if you trust me, you can save yourself.'

She gestured vaguely with her hand; I never knew if in acceptance or regret. Just then, I heard a loud noise downstairs, followed by a shot and a woman's scream. A dark force was storming, beating, and shooting its way from one room to the next.

The dwarf rushed in, even smaller now that the weight of the world was bearing down. He did the most incomprehensible thing: he stuck two fingers into the woman's mouth, as if a treasure were hidden there.

'They're killing all the women, to see if they bleed. Help me get her out through the secret door, here, behind the screen.'

But it was too late: in strode a hooded monk, his white habit stained with blood. The dwarf pushed him and the two tumbled down the stairs. I heard the bell as it rang out against the steps, calling customers who were no longer there.

Two other men, also dressed in white and blood, destroyed any hope of escape. They beat me disinterestedly, their eyes fixed on their prey. I watched them pull the woman from her bed. Her now naked body was perfect but cold, arousing astonishment rather than desire. Our enemies stood in silence, as if the sight had made them forget why they were there. One of them remembered, and slashed her throat with his dagger. It was as if the crime took place in a dream: the slit was devoid of blood, nothing but a line drawn on the blank page of her neck.

'This is her,' one of the penitents said.

They carried her out on their shoulders. Her arms were spread wide, her statuesque pose taking leave of it all.

I wanted to follow them, but a dark mass spoke to me from the bottom of the stairs.

'Don't go into the street. There's a secret mechanism under her tongue to prevent theft, and I activated it.'

I ignored him and went out after the coach. I ran for several feet, only to hear the sound of the wheels as they faded into silence. Then, when it all seemed over, I heard the explosion. Seconds later a flaming horse came galloping toward me. I was able to jump out of the way, and it sped on until it collapsed on the steps of the cathedral.

I followed the smoke and the screams. The detonation had left burning shards of wood and scraps of metal in its wake. One of the monks was still alive, and was begging for water. The others had been blown apart.

I turned back to Bell Manor. Outside, the survivors were crying over the dead. Around them were dog, rabbit, and bear masks strewn by those who had fled. The dwarf – motionless and in a state of shock – was ringing the funeral bell, calling mourners to the final service that would never begin. That sound followed me through the deserted streets and throughout the rest of the night.

The Execution

There was an overwhelming amount of work in the days leading up to the execution of Jean Calas, and I spent morning to night drawing up documents while my fellow calligraphers abandoned the profession, the city, or life itself. The magistrates' unease was reflected in even greater anxiety at the lower levels: secretaries, ushers, calligraphers. A judge's distracted silence, half-spoken word, or hesitant glance would race up stairs, through courtrooms and offices to become a botched document, an ink stain creeping out over a ruling, or a file in flames. My boss, Tellier, assigned me job after job; before the ink was dry on one document, it was replaced by another.

I was always a good calligrapher, but never quick: speed is completely contrary to my profession. Those days, however, I was forced to rush and take less care.

I was the one to record the execution of Jean Calas: his limbs broken with an iron bar, his chest crushed, his death on the wheel. It was hoped he would reveal his accomplices, but he merely asked God to forgive those who had judged him. The closer he was to death, and the more horrific the words were, the faster and more perfect my calligraphy became. It was as if I wanted to distance myself from the torture by taking refuge in the calm formation of each letter. There always comes a time when a calligrapher relinquishes the meaning of the words to focus solely on their appearance, demanding the right to know nothing, to understand nothing, to serenely trace an incomprehensible foreign language.

The story had come to the worst possible end, and there was no longer any reason for me to be in Toulouse. I wanted to return to Ferney and wrote Voltaire for instructions. His reply was alarmingly obscure; I didn't know whether to attribute the confusion to his advanced age or fear the letter would be intercepted. I managed to glean that he had carefully read my reports and concluded the Calas case was part of a more complex set of events, relating to a series of miracles that had occurred in various parts of France. He sent me some money and told me to leave for Paris.

I went to the courthouse to ask for my pay, and told Tellier I would be leaving. He asked me to do one final thing: deliver a letter to the bishop in Paris. The messenger who was supposed to leave that night had gotten drunk and was fast asleep; his horse and carriage were waiting. I felt like an actor who arrives halfway through a performance of an unknown play and is told to faithfully follow incomprehensible stage directions. I barely had enough time to gather my things.

The coach left my lodgings but was soon forced to stop; there was a crowd near the square where we had watched *The Calas Murderers*. I thought there must be an evening show – the dark would accentuate the shadowy story, and hearing voices alone would underscore the horror. But there was no movement on stage, and I found it odd that something you could neither see nor hear would attract so many people. Someone carried a torch on stage, and I recognized the actor who played Marc-Antoine. He was now hanging from a rope, his performance so flawless that his face was blue and his swollen tongue protruded from his mouth.

I saw Kolm on the edge of the throng, where the distracted and the newly arrived listen to hazy, disjointed accounts of events occurring on center stage. I wanted to ask him about the play's ending, but was only able to wave. He, in turn, held up his mechanical walking stick.

Despite the terrible things I had witnessed in Toulouse, I was sad to be leaving. That feeling soon disappeared, however, as if trampled under the horses' hooves. I was only twenty years old, and at that age, the cities you leave behind are erased from memory while those that lie ahead fill your imagination. Now, on the other hand, the only clear picture I have is of the cities I've left, while the more I explore my new home, the more blurred and shadowy it becomes.

PART TWO

The Bishop

The Abbot's Hand

My uncle's house was in absolute darkness when I arrived; he was horrified by unnecessary expenses, and all expenses were unnecessary. The maid had a candlestick, but was forbidden to light it. She held it high, as if it were actually capable of dispersing shadows in hallways crammed with the furniture and paintings that were sometimes received as payment for transport. Identical statues, set in different places around the house, gave guests the impression they were lost in a maze. We finally reached a small room at the top of some stairs. I waited until the maid was gone before I lit a candle, all the while afraid the glare would bounce from mirror to mirror until it found and woke maréchal Dalessius.

Surrounding me were things that had belonged to my dead parents, lost in the sinking of the *Retz* when I was a boy. The ship had earned a place in navigation history: only four days had passed from the time it was launched until it sank. Those objects, slightly damp and mostly broken, looked like wreckage from a ship. But they were the only proof – other than me – that my parents had ever existed. Looking out from a picture in a splintered frame, they were serious and distant, as if they knew what awaited them in the port and the fog.

There was barely enough space for the bed. The room was so disorganized it seemed to hide an agenda: my uncle hoped I would come face-to-face with that sad museum, shed a few easy tears, and run away never to return.

I went looking for him the next morning, afraid I might actually find him. The cook told me he had left early, long before dawn, as was his custom; now he merely watched my every move from an enormous portrait. As I devoured everything the cook set on the table – very little indeed – I studied the message for the bishop. I was tempted to open it, but didn't dare: there were so many wax seals it would have taken days to recreate.

The bishop had retired to Arnim Palace (a Dominican abbey for the last twenty years) when he first fell ill. Other orders were vehemently opposed: they did not want a bishop cut off from the city by high perimeter walls. The Dominicans, however, had known how to negotiate with Rome and became the protective guardians of a bishop ever more saintly and closer to death.

The estate in Arnim was also home to another famous guest: Silas Darel. Although few had seen him, and authorities within the order refused to confirm or deny his presence, it was commonly held that he lived and worked there. Pages written by his hand were highly-prized rarities on the manuscript market and often fetched a higher price than works from the Venetian school of calligraphy. Rumors were rife among my colleagues: Darel was no longer able to hold a quill, he worked with transparent ink, he only wrote in blood. No one knew anything concrete about him. The Dominicans kept him closeted away, like a prisoner, in some secret room in the palace.

I presented my credentials at the door and made it clear I was no ordinary messenger; I was a court calligrapher and was to personally deliver the message to someone in a position of authority. A monk led me up stairs and down corridors to the library.

I had heard of Abbot Mazy; he had recently been involved in a controversy regarding the veracity behind the lives of saints. Mazy held that the only proof of true martyrdom was that the lesson be clear. There was no point in searching for historical truths in far-off times if the message was of no contemporary value; the story itself was to accurately depict events, through what the proponent of the theory called *the moral consistency of the story*. His opponent, a Franciscan, proposed that all martyrology be reviewed to discard any cases in which there were doubts. Mazy responded that faith should always represent an effort; there was no merit whatsoever in believing what is reasonable.

The abbot was pale and his skin so white he seemed to glow in the dark. At fifty years of age, he was at once a boy and an old man. He had lost his right hand when young, and questions about the accident only infuriated him. Sitting at a table in the library, a long, sharp penknife, several quills, and pieces of paper lay in front of him. He gestured to indicate that I should open the message. I used his knife and clumsily cut my index finger.

'There's a postscript. I always start there. People write what's least important in the body of the letter, what's more important they hurriedly note in the postscript, and what's truly essential they never write at all. I see it mentions your skill as a calligrapher. Do you have work?'

'I thought I would apply at the courts.'

'Don't sell your pen so cheaply. Did you know we have our own calligraphy school? Silas Darel is our master, but he speaks to no one: he has kept a vow of silence for the last twelve years. All he does is write, shut away in an office. Have you heard of him? He designed our script.'

We had been taught the Dominican style – too rigid for my taste – at Vidors' School. Easily distinguished by its aversion to curves and constant pressure on the paper to achieve a sense of depth, calligraphy wasn't seen to flow along a page but was more like a laceration. Every dissertation on calligraphy noted how Darel's first profession, as a headstone engraver, had influenced his art.

Legend had it that, on his deathbed, a master calligrapher (whose name no one remembered) asked Darel to carve his tombstone. When he saw Darel's skill, the master initiated him in the mysteries of calligraphy, which dated back to the Egyptian scribes. Such knowledge had been passed from master to disciple for centuries, but only when death was near. The teachers at Vidors' School would laugh whenever older students told this story to impress the novices.

'We sometimes take our seminarians to see Darel,' Mazy said. 'After watching him for a few hours, there are those who run scared and leave the profession altogether, while others discover their destiny.'

'If you have your own calligraphers, how could someone like me be of use to you?'

'We have no shortage of calligraphers, that's true, but they are men of God. I need someone who can do impious work.'

He took the stopper off a Rillon inkwell shaped like a snail, picked up a long quill – more flamboyant than practical – and plunged it into the black ink.

'Where does Darel work?' I asked.

'There's an office at the end of the calligraphy hall, down a few stairs. The entire palace could be his, but he rarely leaves that room.'

'Would I be able to watch him work?'

'When the time is right. Every calligrapher must confront Darel to see whether he made the right choice.'

Abbot Mazy passed me the quill and opened his hand.

'Write your name.'

It was a moment before I understood his instructions. I took his hand, whiter than paper, and slowly, fearfully, wrote *Dalessius*. It looked like someone else's name there. No ink was absorbed by the abbot's skin and the nib was so full that rivulets seeped out from the letters to fill the lines in his hand. As my name grew into something that resembled a drawing in a fortune teller's tract, I could feel the abbot's hand tremble, as if the touch of the pen transmitted pain, pleasure, or cold. He pulled his fingers into a fist and said:

'Now I've got you in the palm of my hand.'

A friend of V.

The abbot told me I had passed his test but didn't explain what my job would be.

'Come see me in a week. I'll have a letter of recommendation for you to start at Siccard House.'

Life at my uncle's was increasingly unbearable. He was always at work, so I could never speak to him, but his presence was made manifest through instructions given solely to inconvenience me: every night there would be new objects in my room, blocking the way, crowding the bed up against the wall. Toys I had given up for lost years ago would come crashing down; a wooden horse knocked me on the head.

A Friend of V.

One night I found a message signed *A friend of V.* on my pillow, asking me to come to Les Cordeliers. I had no idea how it got there, and my apprehension only grew as I walked to the Pension d'Espagne. The door was open but the rooming house appeared to be empty; I went from room to room, afraid I'd be mistaken for a thief, until I found a man in bed, empty beds all around him, with blankets pulled up to his nose. My obvious unease identified me as his guest, and he beckoned me in.

I sat a prudent distance away, afraid he might be hiding his face because of some illness. With the covers still over his mouth, he told me his name: Beccaria. He pronounced it decisively, as if that one word was enough to erase all fear. I had once seen a portrait of Beccaria but distrusted painters, so generous with the distribution of balance and beauty. In any event, the man's face was still obscured, and I was afraid he could be an impostor. Voltaire had written a brief essay praising Beccaria's book – *Of Crimes and Punishments* – but no one believed it was his. That same curse had always plagued Voltaire: his authorship was questioned whenever he signed his work, while every unsigned satire was immediately attributed to him.

'Mutual friends asked me to contact you. They're waiting for news at the castle.'

'And I'm waiting for money. Do you have any for me?'

'I've got nothing to do with that. I'm simply offering to take your message to the border.'

'How do I know I can trust you? Your fame reached the farthest corners of Europe, yet here you are, in a rooming house for the poorest court workers.'

'There are spies everywhere. My enemies hire enemies who hire enemies.'

'Who are they? Are they in the priesthood?'

'I wish. My enemies are people who used to be my friends. They know me and can therefore predict my next steps. I have to become someone else in order to hide, and then I do things I detest. But only as another can I be safe.'

His accent and the blanket over his mouth made him hard to understand, but I soon gathered he was telling me the story of his life. Beccaria had never been interested in justice, the topic that had made him so famous, until, one day, more out of friendship than any real interest, he joined a group of intellectuals from Milan who established a journal called *Il Caffè*.

'I actually liked math, but everyone around me was a writer. I never could stand to hold the pen for long; it made me sleepy. My friends, particularly the Verri brothers, worked tirelessly. I wanted to chase women, go out on the town, like we used to, but the publication was so important to them that I had to keep quiet. They were annoyed by my lack of drive, and Alessandro Verri wound up threatening me: they would kick me out if I didn't get to work. I asked him to give me a topic to write on; he suggested justice. I recalled the walks we used to take, when we would discuss *The Spirit of the Laws* all night long. I decided to maintain the tone of those aimless conversations in my piece. When I started to write, I carried a list of the people executed in Milan as a sort of amulet. Every afternoon, before dipping my quill in ink, I would recite: Massimo Cardacci, hanged; Renzo Zarco, dismembered; Vittorio Lapaglia, decapitated, his remains thrown in the river; and this one hanged as well, and that one put to death on the wheel, then burned at the stake in the square. My friends would laugh whenever I read that list as if it were a spell to give me power over words, but they all encouraged me when they saw that it worked.'

Beccaria jumped out of bed and began to get dressed. He looked like a mere sketch of his own portrait: his clothes hung off him as if he had suddenly lost weight. He moved as if he were sleepwalking.

'I put the book together bit by bit, like a woman sewing a dress out of scraps of material. My friends helped me edit it and kindly gave it to a printer. Friends can be so helpful when they doubt your ability! But as soon as they know what you're worth, they turn against you. There's nothing worse than literary envy. The Verri brothers have slandered and hounded me ever since. Not even the Venetian Council of Ten attacked me as viciously as my old friends! They've accused me of being an impostor, criticized my appetite, my vulgarity, and even taken advantage of one time when I was startled by a spider to call me a coward.'

He opened the trunk and attempted to tidy things; his clothes were dirty and wrinkled, his books missing covers and falling apart.

'Write your message and I'll deliver it,' he said more calmly now.

As Beccaria dressed, I took a quill and ink out of my bag and used the trunk as a writing surface. I started by recounting recent events and then outlined my next steps; fearing the messenger might be a spy, I spoke indirectly, using subtext and subterfuge.

Beccaria would look out the window, leap from one side of the room to the other, stop to listen to footsteps on the stairs. He saw signs of danger in everything, and his fear was so contagious it made my prose even more obscure.

'You've no idea how I've dreamed of going to Ferney. Arriving there will be like crossing the border between my past and my future. What can I take Voltaire? I was thinking about a clock.'

'Anything but. Perk up your ears, go to the theater, stop to listen to what people around you are saying, and then describe all of it, in as much detail as possible. Voltaire has received every imaginable gift, but words are all that interest him.'

My letter never reached Voltaire. Beccaria suddenly changed direction and headed for Milan. It was all the fault of a sick woman he saw on the street. He was so moved by the sight of her that he imagined his own wife ill and destitute, and returned home as quickly as he could. Signora Beccaria was as healthy as ever, but her husband never traveled again. He spent the rest of his life out of the spotlight, as a teacher. He and the Verri brothers never exchanged another word. The brothers had this to say to anyone who would listen: 'Piece of advice? Never help anyone out of their boredom and apathy.'

My letter lay forgotten in Beccaria's suitcase. He discovered it years later and, guilt ridden, sent it to Ferney. It reached me after Voltaire had died, when I was organizing the archives. I had written it in one of my experimental inks, and every single word had disappeared in the intervening seventeen years. Only a few strokes remained, the heaviest ones, that now reminded me of bird tracks in the sand.

Siccard House

The Siccards were a family of papermakers who over the years had expanded into quills and inks. They raised their own geese, a Belgian breed with blue and gray feathers, which they hardened in glass soot heated in an iron furnace. The founder of the family business, Jean Siccard, had died two years earlier, and the business, mismanaged by his son, had been on the verge of closing. In recent months, however, the young Siccard had found his way. Now, the moment a customer walked through the door, there was an array of quills organized in large drawers, sheets of marbled paper, accounting ledgers, hand-drawn staff paper, and Chinese cartographic materials.

When I arrived, an employee was preparing an order for the courts. I showed him the letter from Abbot Mazy, and he looked at me in alarm, possibly because there were other people in the room. He motioned for me to go into the back, in more of a hurry to get rid of me than actually indicate the way. I had no idea what the letter said, or what ruse the abbot had employed to get me hired at Siccard House. I went down the hall, passing an employee up to his elbows in paper pulp, and found a staircase behind a folding screen adorned with Arabic script.

A young man came out to meet me; he was wearing an ink-stained shirt with backwards letters as clearly distinguishable as if it had been used for blotting paper. He skimmed the letter quickly.

'I'm Aristide Siccard, son of Jean Siccard. It was my idea to take the family business in a new direction. You couldn't have come at a better time: one of our calligraphers is sick and another is an hour late. Our messenger can't wait much longer.'

He led me into a small office where a woman was resting on a divan, barely covered by a blanket. She woke up, looked at me, and asked whether I minded if she slept while I worked, assuring me she could doze on her feet.

Hers was the absentminded beauty of someone who has never really looked in a mirror. I was at a complete loss for words as she had let the blanket fall, and I had never seen a naked woman. My only experience came from a certain book of engravings called *Aphrodite's Garland* that had passed from hand to hand through the dormitories at Vidors' School.

Siccard brought me the inks they used (thicker than normal ink to prevent it from running on skin). Aristide began reading the text of the message aloud, while I concentrated on holding my hand still. A calligrapher's life is destined to be routine; whenever anything exceptional occurs, his hand begins to shake and all skill evaporates. Unlike every other artist that leaves a mark and is remembered, this long, laborious wait and inability to rise to the occasion means we as calligraphers fade away, and are ultimately forgotten by History.

As per Siccard's instructions, I began with her upper back. The woman's name was Mathilde, and that was the first thing I tried to forget. She had pulled up her hair – as black as a pool of ink – but it kept spilling down, threatening to smudge the letters. I tried to think about something else, attempted to concentrate on the message, but the rigidity of those words – administrative councils, investments in Dutch notes – was so contrary to the act of writing that it seemed to pervert the technical terms. I tried to let the light that bathed Mathilde's body erase all thoughts. I would look at her as if she were an object, nothing more than a surface, and be somewhat successful as I wrote a *t*, but the curve of a capital *R* would start my hand trembling again.

I refused to give up, and tried to recall the anatomy book that had so disturbed me when I was a student. I wanted to picture the repulsive layers of muscle and bone, but beauty triumphed over my every strategy.

I could hear the worry in Aristide's voice and made one final attempt to improve my nearly illegible penmanship: I imagined my hand belonged to Silas Darel, and was therefore immune to distraction. This thought allowed me to cover areas of a woman's body I was seeing for the first time. It didn't feel like my hand was writing the message; it was more like the words were patiently pushing my hand from letter to letter. My calligraphy looked like someone else's, until it came to the signature, which forged an unknown name and finally reflected an energy and a caution I recognized as my own.

I might not have been as inept as I remember because before she asked me to leave to dress in peace, Mathilde looked approvingly in a full-length mirror and said:

'I never feel naked when I'm covered in writing.'

By the time I finished, my nerves were so frayed that I wandered aimlessly until I was lost on the outskirts of the city. Just when I was about to head back, I saw black smoke spiraling up from somewhere nearby. I thought a building must be on fire but it was a court-ordered burning: books and papers were ablaze as the crowd stared intently at the smoke, as if they could read something in those swirls and lines that I was unable to see. Posted on the wall, a judicial proclamation listed the works that were being burned: it included a satire attributed to Voltaire, in which he ridiculed a recent decree. The paper said nothing about the executioner who had set the pile on fire, but a sketch of a mechanical hand concluded the edict.

Von Knepper's Trail

The watchmakers of Paris were notoriously hard to find. They never set up in a given street, but traveled around the city as if it were the face of an enormous clock and they were the obedient hands. Surrounding them was an assemblage marked by time: almanac vendors, fortune-tellers, and astronomers who wanted their celestial observations to be added to calendars.

I asked around for Von Knepper, whose name had appeared in the letter from Father Razin. No one knew him, but they were so completely unaware of his existence that the very possibility of him seemed to fill them with fear. I asked one after the other, receiving negatives or silence in reply, until one furtively pointed to a woman who was displaying some books on a stone bench.

'Madame Buzot is an expert in the history of machines. She might be able to help you.'

I looked over at the woman wearing a black cloak that revealed only her hands and face, mapped with old scars. I asked the watchmaker about them: their precision betrayed a method, not simply chance or bad luck.

'Madame Buzot was the only female watchmaker in Europe. She was to replace old Van Hals, who was responsible for all the clock towers in Strasbourg. On December 31, 1750, he activated a device to stop the hour hand at precisely twelve o'clock. When Mme Buzot came to repair it, Van Hals was hiding and pulled her inside the clock, intending to kill her. She survived because the mechanism jammed. All of the clocks in Strasbourg came to a halt while she was trapped, and only when she was rescued did time start up again.'

I approached this Mme Buzot. The books open on the bench showed detailed diagrams of cogs, springs, and gears. It was hard not to stare at her scars but I greeted her, commented on her merchandise, and finally mentioned Von Knepper.

'You won't find his name in any book,' she said.

'It's not a book I'm looking for. I want to find Von Knepper.'

'If you knew what you were saying, you wouldn't say it out loud. The makers of automatons have fallen from favor; rumor has it they never existed.'

She began to whisper in my ear. Her many years around clocks had given her words a regular beat, as if each syllable corresponded exactly to a fraction of time.

'Von Knepper was a disciple of Jacobo Fabres and worked with him until his death. Fabres taught him to build geese and flautists, but Von Knepper wanted to make the most difficult piece of all: a scribe. No one knows if he succeeded.'

'Where can I find him?'

'I've heard of an artisan in a dark street, not far from here, who can restore a clock figurine's precise movements. If you buy something, I might tell you the name of that street.'

I asked the prices, but they were all too high – particularly when I had no interest in the topic. Madame Buzot finally pulled a small book with a clock on the cover out of a bag, and asked a reasonable price.

Once I had paid, the watchmaker brought her lips to my ear and told me where I might find him. I glanced at the little book as I listened: there was a drawing of a clock on each page, so if you flipped through it quickly, it looked like the hands were moving.

Everyone around us was gone; the watchmakers had abandoned the place, as if the distant pealing of bells were a summons.

With the little book in my pocket and the street name in mind, I headed to Siccard House, as I did every other afternoon. The more dexterous I became, the more I hoped to postpone the moment when my mercurial position as a spy would force me to leave. My hand no longer trembled, and I had learned to adapt my writing ever so slightly to the pliancy of skin. There were four messengers, and they all liked to converse as they waited for us to finish. Most of all they enjoyed talking about their trips, which sometimes took them far away for weeks at a time. At first I answered in monosyllables, trying to forget the surface under my quill was a woman. Later I intrigued, then amused, and finally bored them with my knowledge of the history of calligraphy. I often think I did some of my best work there, on those words that were inevitably lost between the sheets, with soap and water, or in a sudden rain shower.

Only Mathilde still threatened my calligraphy. I envied the men she was sent to, who would watch her undress, and read the message, late at night, next to a fire. I spent much more time with her than they did, but the fact that she wasn't addressed to me put her out of my reach.

Dussel, a calligrapher from Leipzig, was even more obsessed with Mathilde. He had come to Paris after fleeing his native city, where he was wanted for destroying a printing house. Dussel had belonged to the Hammers of God, a sect that believed the printing press would prevent man from ever discovering the original language, prior to Babel. They saw the printed word as the true Tower of Babel and, using calculations that were incomprehensible to anyone else, established similarities between the types of lead used in printing and the elements the Bible said were used to build the tower.

Mathilde's nakedness was more unsettling to Dussel because he pretended to be pure, while I couldn't have cared less about purity. Mathilde enjoyed this power and used conversation to try and distract him from his perfectly uniform letters. No matter how tense Dussel was when he wrote (and he was often so tense he would fall unconscious when a job was done), he never made a mistake.

Dussel would avoid writing on Mathilde's most secret places, condensing his script so as to finish before the work became unbearably indecent. Mathilde would shift imperceptibly, to force him to use more space, but he never crossed the line he had set for himself. From the office next door, I heard Mathilde issue him an even greater challenge: Since the Bible was the only book young Siccard deemed edifying enough to leave in the offices, could Dussel transcribe the entire New Testament on her body?

Aristide Siccard trusted Dussel, paying him double what he paid me, even though he was no better. In Siccard's mind, unhappiness was sensible, obsession responsible, and misery virtuous.

The Bishop's Silence

I had worked long enough now to report to Abbot Mazy and provide a little false information for a bit of real money. Not one of the messages I had transcribed spoke of the bishop, but as I walked to see the abbot, I invented the words that faraway men had exchanged under cover of anonymity, women, and the night. I crossed palace halls, descended into cellars, and climbed a dank tower, patiently following directions from monks who had just seen the abbot cross palace halls, descend into cellars, and climb a dank tower. After searching for hours, exhausted, I came to a corridor. Mazy was walking toward me, his white cassock dragging on the ground.

The abbot looked at me as if he'd never seen me before. I imagined he must have spies everywhere, and it would therefore be hard to remember all of their names and faces. I told him there was talk of the bishop's abduction, even his death, and that the rumors were insistent.

'Do they mention proof or witnesses?'

'No, Monsignor.'

'Fantasy and rumor are sins the Church has not condemned enough,' Mazy said. 'Come with me and I'll show you the bishop is alive.'

We walked down the corridor; leaves and rain blew in through the open windows. Down below was a geometric garden, where plants and shrubs surrounded deep ponds made of black stone. I asked the abbot whether they raised fish.

'There are some sea creatures that we use to make ink, which we then sell abroad. Darel advised us in this undertaking. Our botany is inspired by calligraphy as well. No strangers are allowed to walk through the garden because of all the thorns and poisons in the species we cultivate. Everything we use to write with can also be used to kill.'

We were approaching a carved door. It was being guarded by a giant of a man, with hundreds of keys hanging from the belt of his green uniform. Seeing us, he nodded respectfully to Abbot Mazy and stepped aside. This set his keys jangling, like bells calling the faithful to mass.

'Signac holds all of the keys to the palace. We've tried to convince him to leave them behind, but he takes them wherever he goes. I trust no one more than good Signac. He's always right where you need him, to open a door or close it forever.'

The guard reached into an inside pocket and pulled out a key tied with a red ribbon, then turned it in the lock.

'The bishop was gravely ill,' the abbot explained. 'When we thought he was about to die, he had a revelation: he would be saved if he took a vow of silence. The Church was forced to renounce his voice, just when it needed it most. Since then, he has only ever communicated in writing.'

'And how long is this silence to last?'

'Until the final silence.'

Mazy opened the door onto a room made of white marble. I stood in the doorway, not daring to approach the man at the desk. He was leaning over a piece of paper, holding a pen with difficulty, as if it were intolerably heavy.

I couldn't see his face. The marble everywhere was like a prelude to the tomb. It was so cold and so white, even in the semi-darkness, that it resembled a grotto carved out of ice.

The abbot pulled back the gray drapes. Light cut a swath through the clouds and stained-glass windows, illuminating the paper. The bishop dipped his pen in the inkwell and wrote a few letters stripped of any adornment. He wrote slowly, as if all action consisted of a series of inaction.

Everything was completely still, except for the bishop's unhurried hand.

The abbot asked me whether the bishop was alive. It was then I understood this was a test, and that Mazy needed others to see what he saw. The bishop looked like a living corpse, but it was true he did move, and even more true that a reply in the negative would not please Mazy.

Without knowing if it was the truth or a lie, I replied: 'The bishop lives.'

Hunched over, the bishop's face was still obscured. Watching people write is always a bit mysterious, as they speak of things we can't see. The abbot gestured for me to leave and pulled the drapes closed, like a curtain coming down on the final act. Indifferent to the dark, and to the performance that had ended, the bishop continued to write.

Kolm's Walking Stick

After Arnim Palace, I went to the courts to ask for Kolm, but no information was provided about executioners for fear of revenge. When I insisted, they let me leave a message in a basket. The note, proposing we meet the next day, fell in among others that looked like they had been there for years, waiting for someone who never came. A rope was lowered down, and the basket was hung on a hook. The messages soon rose up until they disappeared into one of the upper windows.

I waited for the executioner in front of the courthouse the following day. Suddenly, I felt hands around my neck, and my feet left the ground once again. As I fought for air and recovered from his little joke, Kolm told me that someone from the hanged man's troupe in Toulouse had insisted on accusing him. The law had more to worry about than an actor who had taken his role too far, but he had nevertheless decided to leave as a precaution.

The walking stick with the metal fist still hung off his belt. I asked whether it continued to malfunction.

'It destroys everything it touches.'

'I know someone who can fix it.'

'I'm used to it now.'

I insisted; I didn't want to look for Von Knepper on my own.

We walked around behind a church and into a deserted cul-de-sac, until we reached a green door. The owner's name – Laghi – was engraved on the lintel. A carriage clock was visible through the window; on top of the wooden base, a Vulcan was about to let his hammer fall on an anvil. I pulled the bell but no one came. Kolm pounded impatiently on the door.

A maid opened, said it was late and we should come back the next day. The executioner showed her the silver hand, like it symbolized some higher authority. Mechanical artifacts held extraordinary power in that house, and the servant let us in, as if we had shown her an order signed by the king himself. We were led into a cold room that had only one chair. Kolm sat down despondently and left me on my feet to nervously pace. After we had been waiting for a while, I wandered into the next room.

Up against the wall was a chest with dozens of wide drawers, similar to the ones at Siccard House. I opened the first with some difficulty and found a variety of mechanisms and gears. Most were made of metal, but some had been carved out of glass. It was obvious that certain pieces fit together like the parts of a sentence, but no matter how long I studied and weighed those pieces in my hands, I couldn't imagine the grammar that regulated their construction. However, just as an archaeologist may only need to know one word to then decipher an entire dead language, I found something in the third drawer that revealed the whole: sixty-five empty compartments surrounded one glass eye.

There were footsteps and the sound of keys next door. I assumed it must be M. Laghi, the owner, but saw two men come in from outside. I watched them through the half-open door. There was good reason to hide my face as one of them was familiar: the keeper of the keys from Arnim

Palace. The maid stared in terror at Signac's arms and chest. His keys jangled, conveying the sound of authority from heavy oak doors and thick iron grille work.

'Monsieur Laghi won't be long. You can wait for him in the carriage,' the servant said in a quivering voice.

I came out of my hiding place only after they left. Seeing the keeper of the keys had left me shaken. Kolm, on the other hand, sat dozing, completely unaware.

'Let's leave your walking stick. We can come back for it later,' I said, anxious to leave.

The executioner jolted awake and stared at me blankly for a moment. There was no leaving then, as M. Laghi was walking toward us.

He was dressed entirely in black, as if he were going to a funeral, and in his hand was a small chest. Kolm tried to intercept him, holding up his walking stick, but Laghi barely glanced at it. The executioner, used to asserting his authority, was taken aback by the owner's disdain. Laghi was in such a hurry, it was as if he already inhabited the future.

'What do you want? Are you with them?' he asked, gesturing to the closed door and, through it, to the abbot's men waiting for him outside.

114

'I need you to fix this walking stick.'

The artisan took it dismissively. He tested it two or three times and handed it back to Kolm.

'Take it to a watchmaker. I deal with much more intricate mechanisms.'

'I want you to do it.'

Laghi felt the urge to shove the executioner and call for the men outside to come to his aid but hesitated – not out of cowardice, but so as not to make the night ahead any more difficult than it already was. He snatched the mechanical hand from Kolm and took it with him. The executioner shuddered at being so abruptly deprived of his walking stick, as if his actual hand had been taken from him.

Clarissa

The house now seemed like a machine that processed people in and out at the will of some hidden design. I was hurrying to escape it when I saw a young woman looking in a mirror, at the end of the hall: she was an exact copy of the woman from Toulouse.

I ignored the maid's shouts and approached the ghost. She looked at me with wide, staring eyes. Not knowing what sort of sin I might be committing, I kissed the automaton's icy lips. Her teeth cut my mouth, and I was aware of the metallic taste of blood. Hearing my cry, Kolm came with his fist raised, but lowered it immediately when he saw it was only a girl.

'There's nothing to fear. She's not even real,' I said.

Blood suffused the woman's cheeks, dispersing the illusion and the pallor.

'Are you sure I'm not a woman?'

She brought her mouth toward me, and I closed my eyes, expecting to be bit again but powerless to defend myself. Her lips rested softly on mine. If she was one of Von Knepper's creatures, then Von Knepper was a god.

'This is the second time we've met,' I said, 'but the first time, you weren't there.'

She gestured for me to be quiet and led me by the hand to a room piled with broken mechanical toys: Dutch dolls with springs protruding from the head or chest, a blackbird in a gold cage, a soldier missing an arm. There was also a steam-powered wooden horse, a palace being circled by the sun and the moon, and a bronze Medusa that would open her eyes and toss her mane of snakes.

'Are you Von Knepper's daughter?'

'You shouldn't say his name. Call him Laghi; that's what he's known as in Paris.'

I asked about the young woman from Toulouse.

'Is she more beautiful than me? My father made her when I was a child: she was the future image of me.

117

Then she was sold and passed from hand to hand; the purchasers always promised to keep her, but never did, as if she were cursed. Three years ago, my father lost track of her. She's made in my image and likeness, but while I grow old and imperceptibly wear out, she'll never change.'

'If you two were rivals, you won. There's nothing left of her. A secret mechanism under her tongue caused her to explode.'

'What kind of tears do you cry for a dead automaton? When my father finds out, he'll cry real tears. He always loved her better; he thought she was more human.'

'I would never mistake a frigid automaton for a woman.'

'No? You don't even know who I am.'

She brought her hand to my face, as if she were the one wondering about me.

'Don't tell anyone you saw her. There are no automatons in France; there never were.'

'That's what I want to speak to your father about.'

'He won't see you. My father's in grave danger. He doesn't ever let me go out; I'm like a prisoner here.'

'Then I've come to set you free.'

If she accepted, what would I do with her? Where would I take her? Thankfully, she declined.

'The world out there is just another jail. At least in here it's not rainy or cold.'

I looked at the dolls and mechanical toys all around us: everything was broken, nothing worked, and those very defects seemed to be contagious, so that soon we didn't know what to say or how to move.

The Prisoner

I wrote of recent events and my suspicions, and asked my uncle to make sure the letter reached Ferney. My message also asked for money and instructions: I needed to know my words were being heard, that a clear mind was putting the pieces together and arranging my next steps. At the time, it was common for loose pages, found in the bookstores of Paris, to be gathered up and kept in wooden boxes until, at some point, their rightful place was found. It had recently become popular to bind these lost pages, to create a book that jumped from one topic to another. That's how I felt: I was gathering incomprehensible pages, hoping the great reader, sitting next to a window in a parlor at Ferney, would make sense of them.

Every now and then I would hear rumors that Voltaire was in the city, or that he had died, and wonder whether I might be working in the service of a lost cause and for no pay.

In the evenings I would watch the Laghi house, hoping to see Clarissa. I was prepared to attempt a second meeting as soon as her father went out. But when I saw Von Knepper hurry away, carrying his little chest, curiosity impelled me to follow him.

Von Knepper walked without looking back or to either side. His stride was so long I practically had to run to keep up. We crossed over the river and passed through a market, where I nearly lost him among the vendors leaving for the night. He stopped at an iron gate, and I had to step back so as not to be seen. We had come to the cemetery. The guard was expecting him and let him in without a word. I watched Von Knepper walk through the trees and the graves, until he was swallowed by shadows.

I now had to choose between the graveyard and the house, and decided on the latter. The maid tried to stop me at the door, but I shouted Clarissa's name, and she came to my rescue. Once again she led me to the room with the piles of broken toys, Kolm's walking stick now among them.

'I saw your father at the cemetery. Would he be visiting your mother's grave?'

'My mother died elsewhere, and my father never went to her grave.'

'So what is he looking for there at this time of night?'

'I don't know. If you're so interested in my father, why didn't you follow him?'

'Because I wanted to come here.'

'Then enough about the cemetery. Your shoes are already caked in mud. The more you talk, the muddier things will get.'

She offered me a chair with a cracked leg, and I nearly fell off it. She sat down on a trunk. The room was nearly dark. I thought I could hear the whirring of little machines in the corners.

'It's been a long time since I've spoken to anyone. My father isn't much of a conversationalist.'

'They say he's the greatest maker of automatons in Europe.'

'He's made a tiger and a ballerina, and won over the courts of Portugal and Russia. Sometimes I thought all the time he spent around machines allowed him to discover the secret workings of the world, and his every wish was granted. But then automatons went out of style, and now my father isn't moved by art, but greed and fear.'

'What is he afraid of?'

'He's afraid of Abbot Mazy and his calligrapher, who's writing a book that never ends, using his enemies' blood as ink.'

Darkness had filled the space as we talked, pushing us closer together. I reached to put my arm around her, in that cowardly, imperceptible way that tries not to appear deliberate. Clarissa gave no sign of approval or disapproval, and I wondered whether I might have touched her so softly she hadn't even noticed. Emboldened by her apparent acquiescence, I moved closer still. She didn't reject my caresses but she didn't return them either. The things around us gradually began to move: the Dutch dolls and the dismembered soldiers and the little Greek gods all moved. Everything moved but Clarissa, who sat perfectly upright, as if pretending to be made of stone.

Von Knepper opened the door, and I now felt as if I were caught between two wax statues. He stared at me without seeing. He had something to say – he was going to throw me out of his house, maybe even report me to the police – but it was obvious the very thought of speaking to me annoyed him. His coat was soaking wet and his boots were caked in mud. His mind was still elsewhere, out there, among the graves, and not yet fully present. Now that his body was warming up, it was likely his thoughts would return, too.

'My daughter is ill,' Von Knepper said. 'She often falls into this state.'

He passed his hand in front of her eyes. Clarissa didn't move.

'Please don't visit her again. Her attacks are brought on by strangers.'

'But I didn't go near her.'

'You don't need to. Her condition is very sensitive and can detect strangers before they even enter a room.'

'But you have your daughter shut up in here, like a prisoner.'

'It's her illness that imprisons her. If I were to let her lead a normal life, she'd fall into a trance and never wake up. Don't try to understand. Go now, now that you can, now that you won't run into anyone outside.'

I could feel an extraneous cold. It either came from the girl's immobility or the profound impact the night had had on Von Knepper. He crossed the room and, before I knew it, threw Kolm's walking stick at me. The metal hand closed around my throat. If it had possessed its former destructive force, it would have killed me. Instead, all I felt was a slight squeeze that would barely leave a mark.

'Tell your friend I've adjusted the mechanism. There'll be no need for us to see one another again.'

125

The Burial Chamber

Mathilde no longer had any hold over me; Clarissa filled my thoughts as my hand traced letters on a woman's skin. It wasn't my fantasy to write on her, but I imagined she came to my room late one rainy night, and I slowly explored a message written in an unknown language.

Kolm and I met at a tavern frequented by cemetery workers, where I gave him back his walking stick. He asked me how much it had cost; I told him a lot, but he could make it up to me with a little favor. We were free to speak here without fear of being overheard by the indiscreet or spies; gravediggers only ever talked to one another, nothing else interested them. The long isolation they were subjected to by their profession had led them to distort language and create one of their own. References to tombs, darkness, marble, or death couldn't be interpreted literally; they could mean any number of things, depending on how they were combined. The music of that language was at times as dry and deliberate as shovelfuls of earth, and at others vaguely solemn, interspersed with Latin phrases they had learned from funeral inscriptions.

After years of filthy boots walking through, the tavern now simply had a dirt floor. All bags and tools were left at the door. Medical students would come to buy bones, and goldsmiths stolen jewelry.

To reimburse me for the repairs, I asked Kolm to find out why Von Knepper went to the cemetery. It took jug after jug of awful wine before Kolm gave in to my pestering, and grudgingly agreed to help. He led me over to a red-faced man sitting alone, talking to no one. Forlorn in a corner, he was reading and rereading a thick book filled with tiny notations. He would lick his fingertip to turn the page, then point at a spot in the book, as if he had finally found the very word he'd spent years looking for. I recognized him as the guard who had opened the gate for Von Knepper.

'Remember me, Maron? It's Kolm.'

Maron wasn't used to social interaction and was surprised these words were addressed to him.

'I remember you. I thought you'd left us. Why've you come to this place full of undesirables?'

'I was looking for you.'

'Why would anyone want to see me?'

'The key to the cemetery. I want to invite my friend here to a nighttime stroll through the graves.'

'I've opened and closed that gate for forty years, and never lent the key to anyone.'

'We'll offer you a little something as if we believed that were true.'

Obeying the executioner's signals, I put two, three, four coins on the table before he had me stop.

'And we'll give you one more if you let us take a look at that book.'

Maron pocketed the coins. Unlike every other man there, his hands were clean and white, not a mark of any kind. He spoke in a low voice:

'Just a quick look. Don't get it dirty.'

Kolm took the book and handed it to me. I was initially confused and flipped through the pages, more to pretend

I knew what Kolm wanted than to look for anything specific. He whispered that I should pay attention to the most recent burials. Next to each name was a grave site. I studied each line, searching for the lie that twists the stroke, sends it off course, then forces it back to its original form, but only with extreme effort. Kolm thought we should keep Von Knepper's name out of it, in case Maron went behind our backs. It was best if our purpose remain hidden.

The letter *S* in the name Sarras almost seemed to vibrate, calling attention to its deceit.

We took the key, returned the book, and stood in front of the cemetery gates a little while later, well after midnight.

Kolm refused to go in with me.

'I'm an executioner. My deal with death ends under this arch.'

He stayed to keep watch.

I walked past the headstones to where the monuments were erected. It was like being a stranger in a new land, and I tried to form a picture of the place, but the moonlight seemed to move things around. I read the inscriptions looking for the name Sarras. The path led me to the back, where the oldest tombs were, most of them virtually in ruins, and there, at last, I found it.

On top of a small marble palace, an archangel threatened visitors with a broken sword. The rusty lock had been broken long ago. The cold, nauseating air nearly made me stumble and fall down the stairs that led inside.

Using my lamp, I lit candles that on previous nights had spilled down over coffins and altars. Not even in bright daylight would the sight before me have made sense. One of my teachers at Vidors' School, an optician named Mialot, used to give us an exercise: he would show us blurred lines in which a message would be revealed after a while. It wasn't concentration that let you see the hidden words, but a certain inattention achieved only after a great deal of effort. Once the mystery had been solved, it was hard to believe you hadn't seen the writing all along.

The bishop was sitting in a high-backed chair that resembled a throne. He was being supported by ropes that came down from the ceiling and made him look like a marionette. I've finally found the automaton, I thought. Who could mistake that for a real man? He was surrounded by enormous blocks of ice, brought down from the mountains who knows how. The candlelight seemed to imbue him with an extraordinary sense of dignity; the bishop looked like an underground monarch, capable of governing from the beyond. Anyone looking at those ropes wouldn't think they were holding him up, but were how he controlled his administration's strategies and actions.

One by one, the candle stubs were extinguished in pools of their own melted wax. When nothing but the light from my lamp remained, I noticed the shadow of another intruder on the wall.

Taps on the Window

I had no weapon but my iron lamp and held it up toward the stranger to defend myself if he tried to prevent my escape. He was alone and stood perfectly still, as if trying to go unnoticed. Water from the blocks of ice was soaking the soles of my boots and came right up to my foe's feet. He approached slowly, taking care not to slip and fall.

The hood fell back and revealed Clarissa's face. It was one of those moments when you know the world is as it should be, believe everything is good, and you will always be safe. In between half-spoken words, gulps of air, and incomprehensible gestures, I managed to ask her what she was doing there.

'I wanted to see how my father spends his nights. Evidently he's tired of learning from the living, and now takes lessons from the dead.'

The bishop glowered at our hugs and kisses, worried the heat we were irradiating would melt the blocks and cause him to fall.

A gust of wind extinguished the last flame, and the bishop was left alone in the dark. His performance would go on to the very end, when his head would drop, arms would fall, he would abandon what was left of his dignity and collapse with the ice floe. I pulled the iron door closed, and we walked toward the exit.

'What will you do, now that you know the truth?'

'Better yet: What will the truth do with me?'

The tombs looked like forgotten pieces in a bygone game. I asked Clarissa if her condition really did turn her into an automaton.

'That's just my father's imagination. He thinks his inventions and I are related, that we share family traits.'

'But the other night I saw you completely immobile, as if you were asleep.'

'Doesn't everyone fall absolutely still, as if struck by lightning?' she asked. I was unable to reply when she kissed me. 'Who could mistake me for an automaton?'

Kolm was waiting for us outside the gate, but left before we got there, flicking his hand in a gesture of exhaustion, reprimand, boredom. We hurried back to Clarissa's. Though we had witnessed something momentous, we spoke of inconsequential things – the silly conversations sweethearts have. A light was still on when we arrived.

'My father only ever works at night. One day he'll go blind.'

I didn't even glance at the inventor's window; he meant nothing to me right then. I was saying good-bye to Clarissa without knowing for how long. She was part of a mechanism of appearances and disappearances whose frequency I couldn't predict.

Late every night thereafter, I would tap lightly on Clarissa's window, hoping she would open it, but she never came. Perhaps she was sleeping so soundly that nothing could wake her; perhaps her father had discovered her late night excursion and kept her locked away in a room with no windows. The house was dark, except for Von Knepper's study. Night after night, I stayed away from his window. Then, when I had grown tired of waiting, or perhaps because I had decided it was the last night I would keep watch, I peered in through a crack.

All four walls and several easels were covered in meticulous sketches of the bishop's face, neck, and hands in various positions. The drawings were perfect, but the model had imbued them with a truth the artist hadn't noticed: every detail – the shape of his ears, the corner of his mouth, the emptiness in his eyes – betrayed the lines of death.

The window suddenly opened and Von Knepper's face appeared before me, looking pleased rather than angry, as if, on identical nights, he had kept watch hoping to find me.

Fabres' Disciple

'Come in,' Von Knepper said. 'Let's speak one last time.'

He led me through rooms in shadow to the only one with any light. It was clear, from the number of bolts, that I was lucky to be invited in to a place that was off-limits to others. Sketches of the bishop's hands and face were now all around me, as if the figure of the dead man, multiplied so many times, had taken over the room. It was like being inside the bishop's body. Von Knepper had me sit on a hard wooden chair, the one he used when working, and poured me a glass of cognac.

'I was seventeen when I began as Fabres' disciple. I learned everything from him, but while my creatures were imperfect, his seemed alive. The differences weren't visible to just anyone; it was in the subtleties a mother uses to tell one twin from another. I couldn't seem to duplicate a human's unconscious movement. My creatures were too self-absorbed.

'I did have a few successes and even managed to present one of my scribes before the czar. It was to write out a text consisting of 109 words, praising the sovereign, but a faulty adjustment made it knock over the inkwell and the only praise was an ink stain that spread out endlessly. If I was forgiven, it was only because a wise man believed the accident was a sign of the empire's unlimited expansion.

'After that, I put scribes aside and went back to birds and ballerinas and mechanical jungles. As perfect as those toys were, my real ambition lay elsewhere. Those of us who practice this sorcery are obsessed with scribes. The stiller my creatures were, the more alive they seemed. Whenever they moved, a lifelessness would fall over them, dimming the light in their porcelain eyes, reducing them to but a ghost of a ghost.

'Only some of what we know as automaton makers is ever passed on to our disciples. The real secrets take years to come to light and may only come postmortem, like an ambiguous will that can never be clarified. When the disciple is twice what his master was, when the same thirst, the same resentment, the same hate toward the same enemies has rubbed off on him, when somehow he is now the other, only then does he learn the truth. Fabres, who taught me everything, also hid everything from me. When I approached his deathbed to hear the last line in the book he had patiently written on me, all he said was: "You and I are automatons. What need does the world have of us?" And then he died.

'While his other disciples eagerly awaited the reading of the will – which defrauded us all – I hoped for a letter, a paper folded in two, a new type of gear, or the drawings for a mechanism that would allow me to follow his trail once again. Instead, I received a book called *De Progressione Diódica*, a dissertation on the system that reduces all numbers to one and zero. I wasn't particularly fond of math. I thought about selling the book, but it had been damaged and rebound. It was no longer of any bibliographic value.

138

'Months later, one of my cats knocked the book off the top shelf, and it fell on my inkwell, spilling it. That called to mind the scribe that had betrayed me in front of the czar. I flipped through the book without reading it, remembering every second of my failure instead. Sometimes that happens; we don't see the printed word, but only what our mind quickly scrawls across someone else's pages. The morning light fell straight on the book, and I noticed a faint annotation, then another, and another. My master had used the margins to pencil in his spidery inscriptions.'

Von Knepper had already filled my glass three times. I no longer had the strength to even stand. Everything around me blurred together, as if nothing wanted to be separate from anything else. Sober – sober not only that night but always and forever – Von Knepper continued to speak without looking at me. Like an actor, his eyes were fixed on an imaginary spectator, to prevent the audience from distracting him from his lines.

'It took me two weeks to decipher those words and the next few years to turn those ideas into reality. I learned to encode iron plates with the orders automatons need, so all you have to do is change the plate to give them new instructions.'

He handed me one; it contained a series of perforations that created a pattern I couldn't interpret.

'There are words hidden in those holes, and now my creatures seem as alive as Fabres'. But I've reached a point my master never dreamed of: my creature has taken the place of a man.'

'I saw the bishop, a few days ago. He was still working in the dark.'

'That's no longer necessary. Now anyone who sees him up close, in good light, will think he's a real man. My visits to the burial chamber are over. My automaton is more authentic than the ailing bishop, who didn't even look like himself anymore.'

'Now that your work is done, how can you be sure they won't kill you?'

'The machine needs constant adjustments. I'm the only one who can change the instructions, and I'll make sure no one else knows how. I'm safe.'

I had finished the last drop of cognac and was beginning to realize the danger each word entailed. I wanted to ask Von Knepper why he had told me the truth, what he wanted from me. In a fit of optimism, I decided he might have something to offer me. My eyes fell shut for a few

seconds, despite my fear. When I opened them, I heard
Von Knepper answer the question I had never asked:

'There's no need to hide anything from a dead man.'

Mathilde's Foot

Von Knepper seemed a little embarrassed by the chain of betrayals that would lead to my death.

'My daughter told me about you, and your visit to the cemetery. Don't blame her; she wanted me to know she'd gone out, that she could lead a normal life. The poor thing has been so cloistered in our world, she believes these nightly forays are normal. When I found out, I told Abbot Mazy of your recent actions. They don't know your name, but they know to look for one of Clarissa's suitors. Why get you killed? That wouldn't make me happy.'

'What can I do to save myself?'

'Leave Paris and my daughter. It's love that causes her condition. I have to protect her from love.'

'That's impossible. I can go, but someone else will come along, or Clarissa will decide to live her own life.'

'Anything could happen. My profession has taught me a lesson in humility: even the most perfect machines fail, and mechanisms that seem infallible stop working for no apparent reason. No one has yet invented a *perpetuum mobile*.'

'Let me see her one last time.'

'Last times never accomplish anything.'

'I want to tell her that, if I go, it's not of my own free will.'

'She knows. Clarissa knows why you're fleeing. I've told her about your colleague, the abbot's calligrapher. Although, that might not be such a bad end: your blood could become his ink.'

'That's just part of the legend around Silas Darel.'

'I saw it with my own eyes: the mute calligrapher, the thick book, the red ink. Your name and mine are written there, as well as everything we do, maybe even what we're saying now.'

With a wave of his hand, Von Knepper threw me out of his study, and his world. He hurried to slide the bolts shut, as if locking me in a prison made of cities and countries and continents.

I left the house wondering just how grave the danger was. It was a restless night, every sound heralding the abbot's men coming for me. The next morning, I set out for Siccard House to collect my pay, and thus have the means to leave Paris. I walked hand-in-hand with fear: I would look from side to side, and see a foe in every face. It didn't have to be a uniform or a cassock to scare me; an old woman's glance out of the corner of her eye, a hungry dog following on my heels, a boy waving a wooden sword was enough.

Several customers were waiting for their merchandise at Siccard House: an usher, the legal sheets bearing the watermark of blind justice; a priest, a sheaf of parchment; a musician, staff paper tied with blue ribbon. The trafficking of messenger women had served as veiled publicity for the legal, public face of young Siccard's business. I ran into him on the second floor, always industrious and in a hurry, as if fearing his dead father might suddenly appear and demand to see the balance sheet. He asked me about Dussel, but I had nothing to tell him. Dussel and I never spoke; he rushed home after work every day, though no one was ever waiting for him in his rented room. Before heading into the office at the end of the hall, where Juliette was waiting for me, I asked Siccard for the last few days' pay.

'Can't you wait until next week?'

'No. I have an urgent expense.'

'What about tomorrow?'

'It has to be today. The shop downstairs is full of customers. One of them will pay in cash.'

We were repeating a little scene that dated back to the start of the business itself, long before he was born. Young Siccard always paid, but he felt morally obliged to resist a little. That's what his father had done for decades. Aristide walked away with his head bowed, as if he'd been hurt by my words. I went into the last office, said hello to the messenger, and was starting to prepare my inks when Juliette interrupted me.

'The message is for you today.'

She undressed with professional leisureliness. I began by looking for the signature and found the initial *V* on a perfect thigh. Tired of my distant exploits and cryptic messages, my employer was calling me back to Ferney. I would finally leave fear behind and fulfill my calligraphic destiny, that blank page.

I never did read the final lines. There was banging on the adjacent door and the sound of splintering wood, then Siccard's scream, or rather his moan because he tried to scream, but couldn't. I went out into the hall, and Dussel came charging at me, his shirt stiff with dried blood. I thought he'd been hurt and tried to stop him, but he broke free of my grasp and ran toward the stairs. That was the last time I saw him; as usual, he was rushing nowhere.

I looked into the office, impelled by the curiosity that arrives before fear. Siccard had knelt down in front of Mathilde's dead body. Her throat had been slit. For a moment it seemed as if she were covered in ants; tiny letters filled every inch of white skin, including her lips and eyelids, even the spiral of her ears. Customers were coming up the stairs, drawn by the screams and the blood.

Under normal circumstances I would have fallen to my knees, but terror had numbed me to pain or surprise. If I wanted to escape the abbot's men, I would have to leave before the police arrived to interrogate the employees – those on and off the books. Siccard was still holding the bills he had set aside for me. Wordlessly, I tore them from his grasp. He accepted without protest, as if his hands were no longer his own.

Before I set off running, I covered Mathilde's body with a blanket. Only the sole of her foot was left bare. Siccard took it in his hands and gently turned it from side to side, as if afraid he might break it. Then, in a quiet voice, for all of us who were there (for the others who had suddenly fallen silent, as well as for me as I made my way out), he read the final lines from the Book of Revelation.

Flight

I had the money in my hands, and would leave Paris as soon as I gathered my things. Apart from losing my pursuers, I needed distance from Siccard House. As big as Paris may have been, Mathilde's body lay in the office right next door.

I went to my uncle's and began to prepare my inks, making sure the tops were secure so as not to stain my clothes, or worse. Hearing footsteps on the stairs, I thought it must be maréchal Dalessius, invigorated by the news of my imminent departure. While arrivals make some people happy, my uncle liked only departures. Then I heard the sound of keys, like bells announcing a funeral, and grew uneasy.

The giant figure of Signac filled the doorway. Even when still, his keys continued to jangle, shaken by his breath or the beating of his heart. Behind him was another of the abbot's men, as tall and thin as the dagger he was now drawing from its sheath.

Neither one bothered to beat me or threaten me. All they did was ask who had sent me. I didn't say a word: instinct says that if we can only stay quiet enough, we'll be forgotten in a corner. But the dagger remembered and timidly approached my neck. I knew silence was much less dangerous than the truth: they would slit my throat the minute I opened my mouth. All they were waiting for was a word, a name, a signature at the bottom of the document spelled out by my actions.

I coughed, pretending to try and find my voice, and signaled that I wanted a quill and ink. They understood my terrified gestures and were calmed, assuming that anyone willing to write will have to forego babbling and lies. I chose a purple bottle that smelled of mandrake. In his book on the power of plants, Paracelsus asserted that touching a word freshly written in this ink would kill you. According to him, some words were more susceptible to the venom than others. Instead of words, I chose punctuation: I plunged my quill into the liquid, and full stop into the neck of my nearest foe.

The pain was so fierce that, as he brought his hands to the wound, he cut himself with his own dagger; the thirsty metal was finally satiated. Signac lunged at me, brandishing two sharp keys, but missed. The weight of his armor slowed him down, and by this time I was at the door.

I was completely out of breath by the time I reached the Night Mail offices. Behind a dirty pane of glass, a lone man was writing names and dates and destinations in a book. I pounded on the window until he opened it. He must have noticed some resemblance to my uncle because he didn't ask me to prove my identity, at least not right away. Glancing left and right, startling at anything that sounded like metal, I explained my emergency.

As we walked toward the back of the former salting house, the old employee told me his name was Vidt, and said he had known me when I was a boy. He asked, as if in passing, what ship my parents had died on. When I gave the right answer, he quickened his pace, convinced I was telling the truth, and there was therefore no need to fear a reprimand from my uncle.

We crossed a warehouse filled with coffins and came to where the hearses were parked. One was just leaving, and he shouted for it to stop, ordering that another coffin be loaded.

'Who's it for?' the coachman asked with a touch of impatience, as if there were some event in his miserable life that simply could not be delayed.

'Me,' I said.

'You look healthy enough.'

'Not for long if you don't hurry.'

I put a coin in his hand and let money answer any questions he might have.

Vidt insisted I look like a passenger and so powdered my face. It was a much thicker substance than the one favored by nobility and the bourgeois. I looked at my reflection in the hearse window: anyone who saw me would be certain that life had left me.

We put the coffin in the back and, not without some difficulty, I crawled inside. The coachman was kind enough to put a blanket under my head. I settled in, shut my eyes, and the coffin lid was closed.

The End of the Trip

It was the worst trip of my life, in a life of nothing but terrible trips. Every stone on the road was a punch to my back, every corner absolute torture. Whenever the carriage stopped because of an obstacle or a checkpoint, I wondered if the price on my head might be high enough for the coachman to turn me in. But as soon as Paris was far behind, my coffin was opened to the cold morning, and the driver handed me the reins so he could get some sleep.

We came to an abandoned farm in the middle of a rainstorm. The coach was heading straight on, to the north; I was to continue to Ferney on foot. I walked beneath gray trees and crossed a stone bridge over a stream. With every step I grew weaker; I was exhausted and running a fever. The birdsong was dirgelike, making the trees and the sky even darker, pushing my destination farther away. By the time I reached the castle, I was unable to even say my own name.

I was given a bed and dry clothing, but my request to see Voltaire was ignored. That section of the castle was undergoing renovations so I was moved, bed and all, from one place to another all night long. I went to the kitchens, the foul-smelling cellars, the halls where the clocks were tested (and where there was no way to tell the time because each one was different). Sometimes I was left with other servants who were recuperating from an illness. There was no way to obtain any information: the sick speak an incomprehensible language that no one has any interest in answering. The domestic staff who moved me were terribly somber; I wondered if it was because they didn't know how to treat me (a little less than a gentleman, a little more than a servant) or because they knew my prognosis was uncertain, and carried my bed with funereal solemnity.

The trip wore on, the trip never ended, all through a night that stretched out through rooms and parlors, up and down stairs. Nothing stays still while a fever lasts. My travels ended at the entrance to Ferney theatre, whether on orders from my employer, by chance or mistake, I never knew. Unsteady on my feet, pale, but no longer feverish, I crossed a dark room, like a sleepwalker, amid Sicilian and Japanese puppets, stuffed crows, and the copper frame for a Chinese dragon.

I pulled back the curtain and appeared on stage, like an actor who has arrived late to a performance and forgotten his lines. There was Voltaire – although at first I thought it was an actor portraying him: his decrepitude was so pronounced it suggested theatrical trickery. Others were there as well, spectators and performers, who looked at me in surprise. Once the astonishment had passed, I heard Voltaire say: 'It's my calligrapher, back from his mission.' He said it as if those words brought a long comedy to an end. I heard the applause and felt I was back, at last.

PART THREE

The Master Calligrapher

The Wait

Light shines in through the dirty window, falling on the page, and I watch my hand tremble on the coarse paper. I have learned to turn uncertainty into flourishes. You have to let the ink flow, the hand run toward the next word and the next, never stopping to consider an error. Once doubt begins, it takes over; like the Vatican calligrapher who hesitated over whether to write Pope Clement VI or Clement VII, and then whether it was Clement at all, and finally distrusted every word and never wrote another in his life.

The shaking in my right hand isn't simply a matter of age; it's a symptom of Veck's syndrome (named after Karl Veck, calligrapher to the Habsburgs). Those of us in the profession for decades find our hands acquire a certain independence, and often, when we want to write one word, something completely different comes out. They say that, even in sleep, when Veck was handed a quill, he would quickly write a word or sometimes a whole phrase; the meaning was always obscure, and later, when awake, he would try in vain to interpret it.

Sometimes my hand writes an involuntary word; that's why these pages are filled with corrections. I used to hate imperfection, but I've learned to recognize blots and rewrites as one of the many forms our signature takes. Nothing they taught me at Vidors' School is true. The best calligrapher isn't the one who never makes a mistake, but the one who can draw some meaning and trace of beauty from the splotches.

An abundance of work forced me to interrupt this recollection, but I'll leave this frozen room now, cross the ocean and time, and once again appear on that stage at Château Ferney. Around Voltaire, apart from the usual visiting sycophants, were two women – one older, one younger – who I guessed were mother and daughter. Voltaire was telling them how to portray the Calas drama with passion and rigor.

'It's easy to move the people – they weep at anything – but it's much more complicated to move a court. Don't cry openly. Hold back your tears. Let them spill out against your will.'

The women meekly accepted Voltaire's directions, and I was amazed there were still obedient actresses anywhere. Surely they must be Swiss. Taking advantage of the distraction I had created, they stepped aside to rest for a moment. I asked Voltaire what play they were rehearsing.

'The most difficult of all to perform: Jean Calas' widow and daughter are preparing to visit the courts of Europe in search of support for their cause. I want them to say just the right words, without looking foolish or overacting.'

Hearing who they were, I was about to confess I had been in Toulouse when their father and husband was martyred, and had been to their looted house. But something stopped me: I think they were comfortable playing that theatrical game, hiding behind their roles, and didn't want to be reminded they were themselves.

'It should be enough to tell the heartfelt truth,' I said quietly.

'The heart and the truth make unlikely bedfellows. Our enemies are staging grand performances so we must perform as well. Drama is everywhere but in the theater these days; entire cities are the stage.'

I found myself searching for my place as calligrapher over the next few days. Whenever I found work or tried to organize the archives, Wagnière would reassign the task, promising that Voltaire had other plans for me. Where once I had been a part of castle life, I now felt there was no place for me. I became a ghost; no one would even turn to look at me when I came into a room. I sometimes heard my story as if it were another's. Secretaries, cooks, servants, even the travelers who came to see the genius of Ferney were all commenting on my adventures. These stories were like legends, passed from person to person until distilled. No one could believe that I, an insignificant calligrapher, was the protagonist of such events, and would only listen to me if I spoke as if it had happened to someone else. I existed in third person.

I wrote the final account of my time in Paris and waited in vain to find Voltaire in his study. Business consumed his afternoons, requiring him to make hasty decisions regarding his clocks, his crops, and his foreign investments. I would slip my reports under his door, never knowing if he read them or burned them.

One morning Voltaire himself came to my room and led me to his study. He began by telling me of his aches and pains, but I wasn't worried: his suffering had kept him in good health for years. Then he showed me the stack of pages I had sent. He had made notes in the margins, most of them question marks.

'I've read and reread your reports, written with incomparable incompetence. Despite all the errors, I was able to come to one conclusion: the Dominicans are preparing to take advantage of the void being left by the Jesuits. They've concealed the bishop's death in order to hold on to power. As long as the comedy of the automaton lasts, their hold will remain firm. They are behind the plague of miracles that's storming France; poor Jean Calas was just one more of their victims. That's why I need you to go back to Paris.'

'I'd rather stay here. Your correspondence must be awfully behind...'

'My true correspondence consists of the two messages I'll send with you. The first is for the printer Hesdin, to be published as soon as possible and without my signature. The second is for the bishop. There is a papal delegation coming, and the bishop will confirm the Dominicans' power. You must convince Von Knepper to change the text.'

I pleaded not to be sent to Paris. I was afraid; all I wanted was a simple position at Ferney.

'You'll travel under an alias. In any event, I don't have anyone else to send. Wagnière is too old; I say a teary good-bye every time he goes to a distant wing of the castle, unsure whether he'll make it back alive. I'm not asking you to do this for honor, or to champion an idea you may not share. I only ask that you obey the universal sense of greed: from now on, you will be official calligrapher of Ferney, and your pay will be commensurate.'

I placed money and danger on an imaginary scale that leaned toward precaution. But then I thought of Clarissa, who I missed so dearly that distance actually brought her closer. I imposed one condition on going: a workshop in which to make inks and the right to sell them.

'That could be quite a profitable business,' Voltaire said. 'If we sell clocks to the Turks, why not ink to the French?'

Given Voltaire's advancing age, failing memory, and proximity to death, I drew up a contract. He signed it with a look of reproach, as if disappointed by my lack of faith in his word, his faculties, and his health. I was to leave for Paris in a week. In the interim, Voltaire would closet himself away to prepare the messages I was to deliver. While I refused to get up in the morning or think about my upcoming trip, he would rise early, leap out of bed, sometimes even do a little jig before sitting down to write, as if, from somewhere, he could hear music playing. It wasn't the music of planets or the discovery of some hidden harmony in nature, but the sound of the world that made Voltaire dance.

Anonymous Libel

My break ended and I went back to writing, not with quill and ink but my footsteps and the dust of the road. As soon as I arrived in Paris, I went to find the printer Hesdin, who had worked for Voltaire on previous occasions. His address was on a piece of paper that had been soaked by the rain, and the street name was now nothing but a few faint blue lines. Thankfully, almost all of the printers lived in Les Cordeliers and Hesdin was well-known; I soon found his shop, not far from the Comédie-Française.

I didn't go straight in; there were suspicious-looking people all around, and I wondered whether Abbot Mazy had already heard I was in Paris. But those men with faces obscured, lurking on corners and in doorways, weren't interested in me. These were playwrights in a city so over-run with them that theaters had barred them entrance; they already had enough plays to stage until the end of the century. The new tragedians would prowl around, waiting for any opportunity to slip into the theater. Once inside, they would hide until they could leap on the stage manager or director. Some would even threaten suicide if their work wasn't read immediately. None of this seemed like a problem at the time, but now, looking back, I think it was the ferment for everything that happened later. The Revolution was led, primarily, by frustrated writers, and their literary jealousies and failure to make it onto the stage were what led to the Reign of Terror.

Inside the print shop, an assistant was turning the press. When I asked for Hesdin, I was taken into the back, where a white-haired man was painting gold letters on the cover of a book. Tottering stacks of them were all around.

'Where've you come from?' he asked. 'It looks like you're being followed by a cloud of dust.'

'I've come from Ferney, sir.'

'Then you're not only being followed by dust but problems as well.'

The only chair was covered in books, which Hesdin brushed to the floor. I knelt down to pick up a copy of *Varieties of Calligraphy* by Jacques Ventuil, with twelve illustrations by the young Moreau.

'Does that interest you?'

'I'm a calligrapher.'

'Then do me a favor and take it. I only sold thirty-seven copies. I've fonder memories of books that have been burned than those that were an absolute failure. At least a banned book doesn't take up space. Look closely, that's Baskerville, the print type vaguely reminiscent of the human hand. Baskerville was a calligrapher before he became a printer, and wanted to acknowledge his old profession.'

Hesdin stopped what he was doing to fetch a jug of wine, some bread and cheese. I told myself to eat slowly so as to interject a friendly comment every now and then, but devoured the food without a word. In the meantime, Hesdin spoke.

'On page 108, there's a story about a Chinese calligrapher who was to transcribe a long poem arguing that calligraphy was imperfect. The order came from the palace, and the calligrapher felt a great weight of responsibility.

If he used all his skill to perform the task, the contrast between the subject of the poem and its transcription would be obvious, and he'd have sinned by calling attention to the art of calligraphy over poetry. However, if he decided to write with an unsteady hand and create artificial imperfections, he ran the risk of being fired as palace calligrapher. With the blank page in front of him, brush in hand, the calligrapher thought and thought, until he came upon the solution. He wrote the most beautiful ideograms ever, but when he reached the complex character for *calligraphy*, he lightened his stroke, as if, in reading the poem, he'd been convinced by the poet's argument, and begun to doubt. And so he gained the emperor's favor.'

Hesdin fell silent, waiting for me to finish chewing and explain why I was there. I reached into a bag I had hidden under my shirt and pulled out Voltaire's manuscript. Hesdin sighed deeply.

'Under what name is it to be published?'

'No name.'

'A name can be an alias and we never know who the author is. The minute it's anonymous, however, all doubt is erased: we immediately know who wrote it.'

Hesdin read the tale out loud, while I finished off the last of the bread and wine. The story had seemed innocent enough when I transcribed it from Voltaire's illegible script, and I'd paid little attention: it was just another of his whims, a show of his excessive faith in the power of words. But the printer read it with an air of mystery, as if it were full of questions and secrets. The story was lost over time. Fearful, Hesdin printed only a few copies and not one survived, not even in Kehl's seventy volumes. I only have a vague recollection of it, which I ineptly write below, for the sole purpose of helping you understand subsequent events.

The Bishop's Message

Early in the sixteenth century, the priest Piero De Lucca found volume five of *Mechanical Alchemy* by Johannes Trassis in the library of his monastery. The other four volumes had been lost a century earlier. When he finished reading the text – which he knew was banned – De Lucca began to build a creature made of metal and wood in the cellar.

He worked for an entire year in absolute secrecy. He became known among the other priests as a loner. When finished, his creature learned to walk and to stammer a few words in pure Latin, in a monotonous, metallic voice.

It could give simple answers, but whenever the question exceeded its ability, it would reply: 'I cannot be certain of the answer in that regard.'

De Lucca was amazed by his work. For months he had thought of nothing but its construction; now that it was done, however, he began to consider his pride and wonder whether the creature might be an instrument of Evil. He decided to ask it, and, as on so many other occasions, it replied: 'I cannot be certain of the answer in that regard.'

The priest decided to consult a higher authority. He sent the creature to Milan, with a letter for the archbishop. In it, he asked his superior to carefully study the messenger and reply as to its nature.

Years went by without any word from the archbishop. The priest would sometimes think fondly of his creature, and wonder where it might be: if it was living the life of a common man, if it was corroding at the bottom of the river, or had been burned as a heretic. He could have taught it so many things, but had needed to know whether he had done right or wrong. And so he was damned to wait for a reply.

Now old and infirm, Piero De Lucca told his confessor about his dilemma. He told De Lucca to travel to Milan immediately, so as not to risk dying in doubt and in sin.

The archbishop had by then been succeeded three times (once because of a poisoning), but De Lucca still hoped to find an answer in the underground city of the archives.

Piero De Lucca made the trip. At over eighty years of age, he was exhausted by the time he arrived. He was given a small room next to the cathedral. When the time came to meet with the new archbishop, De Lucca was so weak he was unable to get out of bed.

The thought of dying without an answer pained him. Seeing him so fragile and distraught, the other priests interceded with the archbishop, asking him to go to De Lucca.

Piero De Lucca lay dying when the archbishop came to see him. Full of interruptions, repetitions, and omissions, the priest told the story that had brought him to that dark little room. He begged for an answer to his original question. That answer came at the very moment of death, when he heard the archbishop say: 'I cannot be certain of the answer in that regard.'

'I'd rather the action take place in some Oriental palace, with a caliph or a mandarin instead of an archbishop,' Hesdin said. 'The Egyptians, Arabs, and Chinese never come to complain.'

'It's fantasy. Automatons. Magic. Nothing real.'

'I don't see anything wrong with it either, but that means very little. In this profession, you get used to reading into things. It's only when a book erupts in scandal and flames that we printers realize what we've published. In any event, leave the text with me. I'll understand one day. After all, there's no better way to read a book than by the light of a bonfire.'

The Human Machine

I took a room at the Auberge du Poisson, under an alias, and slept for fifteen hours. When I awoke, I began to think about my future. It had been easy to devise plans and make decisions on the trip to Paris; from far away, cities are like toy towns, where everything is easy, close, and possible. It was only when I got to Paris that I remembered cities are full of obstacles.

There was only one way to make Von Knepper change the message: I had to take Clarissa. With my face obscured by a cloak and hat, I went to the house to spy on its inhabitants. There were signs of decay on the walls and windows, and the house seemed to age as I watched;

a few more minutes and I would witness its collapse. My eyes were tired, and tiring everything they saw. I waited anxiously for Von Knepper to go out, called by some urgent obligation. But now that his appointments with the bishop had ended, there was no reason to leave home. Everything he required was inside those walls.

While Von Knepper needed solitude and obsession in order to think, all I needed were long walks and momentary distractions. I found something of interest in every passing conversation; every notice in the street forced me to stop. There were words all around me, and I paid attention to each one, as if the city were an enormous book that could inspire my next steps. And so, in reading the words that came at me with no rhyme or reason, I discovered a poster for a book auction.

Tramont, whose appetite for books was as voracious as the Duke de la Vallière's, was putting some up for sale. His collection was so enormous that, from time to time, Tramont was forced to part with duplicates or books that were no longer of interest simply to clear a path through his house. At the bottom of the notice was a list of the most important volumes in the lot: number three was a copy of *The Human Machine* by Granville. This was an extremely rare book. Fabres, Von Knepper's mentor, always swore there was absolutely no proof that Granville's dissertation ever existed. I can assure you it did: I saw its pages and its engravings, and I saw how a copy sank in the waters of the Seine.

I tore the announcement off the wall and left it under Von Knepper's door. Fate would take care of the rest.

It was five days until the auction. Von Knepper set out for Tramont's house at the exact time it was about to start – as if he had only just decided to go. He walked straight past without seeing me: all that mattered to him was in the past or the future, and anything along the way belonged to the vulgar present. I waited a few minutes, in case he changed his mind, and then approached the house.

I had brought enough money to bribe the maid; as soon as she opened the door, I asked for Clarissa.

'You should know where she is,' the woman said.

'Why me?'

'Monsieur Laghi told me you took her. We haven't seen her in six days now.'

I couldn't believe Clarissa was gone and strode to the back of the house. The maid didn't bother to stop me: there was no one for her to protect.

'How did she disappear? Was she taken by force?'

'It was the middle of the night. If you don't have her, then she left on her own, tired of being overprotected. Monsieur Laghi hasn't been able to sleep since. I hear him pace the room all night long, repeating the same words: *I know everything about machines and nothing about people.*'

The auction was running late, and had just started by the time I arrived. Books were piled in great, tottering stacks. Since the nobility had acquired a passion for antique books, it was best if they looked truly old. Everyone knew that, a month before an important auction, they were locked in a trunk with Amazonian spiders, to be enveloped in layers of cobwebs. The volumes were never cleaned because the accumulated filth confirmed antiquity. Publication dates simply weren't enough: collectors liked to feel their treasure had been snatched from oblivion seconds before it came into their hands. Thus, every time the auctioneer presented a book, a cloud of dust would rise up, causing the first few rows to erupt in coughs and sneezes.

Gathered in the Tramont house were the most notable collectors from Paris, as well as dealers from Antwerp and

Brussels who were trying to blend in. A few stood alone, but most were in groups of two or three. Though from the outside they may have looked like one big family, they were in fact eyeing one another suspiciously: each belonged to a rival religion and what one considered gospel was heresy to another. Those who chose books based on their bindings would laugh at those searching for Elzevirian or Roman type; experts in typography couldn't understand what others saw in vignettes and bronze engravings; academics in search of Latin classics despised a love of a book's material qualities, aspiring to more ethereal volumes instead.

The auctioneer had saved *The Human Machine* until the end. By this time, half of the buyers had already left. A bookseller from the Pont Neuf opened with a laughable bid. Von Knepper raised his hand, and this was echoed weakly by his competitor. The game continued for no more than three or four amounts, and the book was soon Von Knepper's for no trouble and little cost. Having been rebound, it was of no bibliographic value. It was only of interest because it was so rare.

I sat down next to Von Knepper as he held the acquisition limply in his hands. All interest had evaporated now that it was his. The hate I expected to see in his eyes when he saw me was in fact something worse: hope. This was no longer a man to be feared, but an old man begging forgiveness without knowing why. The last few days had filled his voice with pleading:

'Where's my daughter?'

'I don't know. You know very well I had to flee.'

'If it wasn't you, then who?'

'The abbot's people?'

'They have me firmly in their grasp; they don't need my daughter. In any event, she left of her own free will. She could be anywhere in the city now. She doesn't know a thing about life; she doesn't know how to work. How will she survive?'

The auction had ended. All of the collectors were leaving, treasures in hand. I followed Von Knepper out.

'I'll look for your daughter.'

'And what's your price if you find her?'

'You're worried about price? I thought all you'd care about now was Clarissa.'

'If the cost for finding my daughter is to give her to you, that's too high a price. I don't make those kind of deals. At most, if you're patient, I can make you a copy.'

'I'll look for her first. Then we'll talk price.'

We had come to the Seine. Von Knepper flipped through the book by the light of the moon, stopping at the engravings, studying the binding.

'At least I directed you to a good deal,' I said by way of good-bye.

'This book? I know it by heart. It doesn't interest me in the least.'

'Then why did you buy it?'

'To destroy it. The last thing a maker of automatons needs is for this sort of information to get out. Secrets must be kept.'

He threw the book, as far as he could, and it splashed into the river.

The Halifax Gibbet

I looked for Kolm at the courts by the usual method of leaving a message in a basket, which disappeared into one of the upper windows. A crumpled piece of paper was sent back down, telling me to meet him the next night in a classroom at L'école de Medécine.

No one stopped me at the iron gate or among the columns. I walked down a corridor that began in half-light and ended in absolute darkness. Kolm was waiting for me, part way down, at the bottom of some stairs. All around him were large portraits of famous doctors; despite the stains on his overcoat, it was as if posterity had rubbed off on Kolm as well.

179

He gestured for me to be quiet, and I followed him, up stairs and down halls, to a room with piles of murky jars, wax sculptures of sections of the brain, and skeletons enveloped in cobwebs.

Kolm sat down at a long table, covered in dozens of yellowing sheets containing the type of meticulous drawings we had become used to in the *Encyclopédie*. But these were old, the edges and folds ravaged by time. They were highly detailed designs for machines whose purpose only became clear after careful examination.

Leaning over, studying the diagrams intently, Kolm was so different he seemed like an impostor.

'Why are we meeting here and not in the square? What are you doing at the school of medicine, with these old illustrations?'

'We're in danger apart, but together we're dead. Here, in this room, we can talk without fear, without anyone seeing us, away from the machinations of Abbot Mazy. Look at everything around us: old, forgotten things. If a person hides among them, he'll be forgotten, too.'

'I'm surprised they let you be here. You're not a doctor or a student.'

'One of the professors has a job only I can do. He

wants to put an end to executions that become torture, because of incompetent executioners. He's searching for a machine as perfect as the best executioner, who takes life without evoking tears or screams.'

I looked at the plans more closely and began to understand. A sword, made heavier by an oversized hilt, slid down two vertical rails. . .

'. . . until it severs the medulla,' Kolm explained in a pedantic tone I'd never heard. 'It was invented by a Hungarian engineer, who tried it on his wife. He said it was an accident but no one believed him, and they executed him with it. It was never used again.'

Kolm rummaged for a sheet that was underneath the others.

'Look at this one. The offender is dressed in metal armor. He looks like a warrior ready for combat, only his enemy is the sky: an electric current travels down from a kite flown through a lightning storm. Death is certain and quick, but the weather isn't.'

In another illustration was a huge ax that hung like a pendulum over the victim, in this case a woman whose black hair seemed to have a life of its own. A second drawing showed her headless.

'A Spanish invention used by the Inquisition in the sixteenth century. No matter how heavy the ax is, because it cuts on a diagonal, it rarely detaches the head completely. Now I'll show you my favorite.'

This wasn't a plan, but an old engraving; it showed a simple structure, just two rails that a blade traveled down.

'The Halifax gibbet, used in England in the sixteenth century, apparently with excellent results. I've almost decided on this model. It won't be hard to build: all you need is wood and a blade, and enough lead to make sure it drops fast and hard. If it works, there'll be no need for executioners; anyone will be able to kill. It's a shame: us old executioners, with our knowledge and our customs, will disappear forever, replaced by clerks who simply have to pull a rope. We'll be forgotten, like calligraphers.'

Kolm was already reaching for more diagrams to show me; I had to interrupt his explanations.

'I didn't come looking for deadly inventions but advice. Clarissa Von Knepper has disappeared. I told her father I'd find her.'

'And why did you promise him that?'

'There's something I have to do, and he's the only one who can help me.'

'Not the bishop again? I hope you don't find her then.'

Kolm looked behind a statue of Hippocrates, in among anatomical specimens, for a bottle of liquor that he set down in front of me. It was sweet but strong.

'Drink and forget. The work you do is unsavory, and I need an assistant. I promised the doctor he'd have his machine in a few days.'

'How will you test it?'

'There's never any shortage of volunteers here.'

'I can't help you, Kolm. I've come a long way to finish a job.'

'A job that will finish you. Well, if that's what you want. . . But bear in mind, this doctor pays well and he doesn't have any significant enemies, yet. Your employer, this Voltaire, on the other hand. . .'

With a look of disappointment, Kolm turned back to his plans and pulled out a map.

'That's not a machine; it's Paris,' I said.

The city was so vast, so full of streets and names, it seemed I'd never find something as small as a woman in it.

'A brotherhood of heretics with ties to smuggling – they called themselves the Syracusans – would use the city in their executions. Whenever they suspected a brother was going to leave the sect, they would sentence him to death, but believed the city always had the last word. One of them would take the role of executioner and wait in a room until midnight. The offender, who didn't know his fate, was told to cross the city and get to the appointed room. If there were no problems along the way, he'd arrive thinking he'd completed his task and would be pardoned, when in fact, the moment he opened the door, he'd be executed with a Norman sword. However, if traffic or other obstacles stopped the offender, forcing him to detour and delaying him, he'd be saved.'

Palaces, bridges, churches, cemeteries. It took my finger seconds to trace a quiet street as easily as another where I'd have been killed for merely setting foot.

'Where in this city could a young woman hide?'

'So you're really going to look for her? You've already had to escape once. Maybe, like the Syracusans' victims, an executioner is waiting for you in a darkened room.'

The liquor seemed to boost my spirits after a while. It simplified the city map, erasing entire streets and neighborhoods. All I had to do was turn a corner to find Clarissa, to save her, and myself.

'Check the convents,' Kolm suggested.

'I know she wouldn't go there. She's had enough of being cloistered.'

'What does Von Knepper's daughter know how to do?'

'Nothing. Absolutely nothing.' I thought for a moment and corrected myself. 'She knows how to do one thing: stay still.'

With the nearly empty bottle in his hand, Kolm pointed to Hippocrates:

'Then ask the statues. They know the secret.'

The Life of Statues

Every Tuesday morning models would gather in the basement of the Académie des Beaux-Arts in search of work. Three big iron stoves tried in vain to heat the room, where the cold seemed to come not from outside but from the statues forgotten in the dark. Those sculptures, once proud exhibits and then inconvenient obstacles, were pushed by the whims of art down into the underground world. Every now and then an expedition would arrive: critics or sculptors would decide to bring back a former style, or a forgotten artist, and archangels, Madonnas, or Greek gods would rise up to the surface again.

The youngest women came from the countryside or abroad; rather than showing any conviction in their new line of work, their bodies seemed to curl into question marks as they undressed near the glow of the great stoves. There was a Chinese folding screen, red lacquer with silk panels, but no one bothered to use it; the drawings made it seem much more indecent than nudity itself.

I had managed to blend in with those who came to the basement in search of models. The young women displayed their figures, some opulent and others angular, while the artists would judge and perhaps propose a deal. If the day's wages were acceptable, the girls would leave with the painters.

There was something odd about the way almost everyone dressed that made them look foreign – except the foreigners, who tried to look Parisian. Everyone came down the stairs silent and alone, but soon began animated conversations with one another and occasionally with the models. They boasted of their latest assignments: a cameo barely whispered, a virgin for a chapel exclaimed, the portrait of a certain countess bellowed. Those with money would soon come to an arrangement and leave with the chosen model; the others, outdone,

would quietly criticize the women who were now beginning to dress.

'I need a model who's not too imposing. She needs
to be more of an outline; she should lack a little defini-
tion,' said one who looked extremely young, almost a boy,
dressed in every piece of clothing he could find.

'You want a model who's a little blurry, like when you're
drunk? Well, that's easy enough to achieve, my young
Arsit!' said his friend, a tall man with enormous hands
who was surreptitiously sketching as he talked. He was
using the girls without having to pay a cent, but his hands
were so big it was impossible not to notice. 'Look at that
one, with the red hair; she's perfect for a Gorgon.'

'They were better fed last year, Gravelot.'

'You weren't even born last year.'

Arsit ignored him and tried to deepen his voice:

'They don't know how to be still. Do you see them
moving, Gravelot? What would Mattioli say if he were
here.'

I asked who Mattioli was.

'Guido Mattioli, the sculptor. You haven't heard of
him? Where are you from?' the boy asked in disbelief.
'You should read his book *The Life of Statues*, instead

188

of freezing to death here. Until you have, you won't understand a thing about models. Mattioli is extremely demanding when it comes to choosing his muses: he won't tolerate the slightest movement.'

'To test them, he smears their breasts in honey and releases a swarm of bees: a real model must be able to remain indifferent,' Gravelot said, still drawing. The women who were left had now recognized his strategy and were hurriedly dressing.

'Before working on a sculpture, the model herself must be a statue,' Arsit explained. 'In his book, Mattioli says: you must wrest the statue that's in the woman to then wrest the woman hiding inside the marble.'

'Where can I find Mattioli?' I asked.

'Do you want him to teach you? He doesn't take students.'

The boy painter smiled arrogantly. He liked knowing what others didn't.

'I'd be happy just to watch him work.'

'I've never seen him, but they say he lives in a house at the end of rue des Cendres. Every now and then an outing is organized: the artists all file out of here on foot, watch him work through a window – never daring to knock on his door – and then they all leave. How many times have you gone to see him, Gravelot?'

'Three. The first time, Mattioli threw water at us; the second, rocks; and the third, a dead rat.'

'And you, Arsit? Haven't you ever wanted to see him with your own eyes?'

'Let me offer you a piece of advice,' the boy painter replied gravely. 'Keep your ideals where they are, just out of reach.'

We were the last ones there. Gravelot, with his enormous hands and feet, clomped up the stairs. Arsit stayed behind.

'What about you? Aren't you coming?' I asked.

He didn't reply, just turned his head and disappeared between a lion and a virgin with outstretched hands.

Gravelot took me by the arm.

'Leave him be. Arsit lives here. He was abandoned as a child and grew up among these statues. He rarely comes to the surface. Sometimes I bring him a plate of food and leave it on the stairs, as if he were a stray cat. Every Tuesday, I shake as I come into the basement, worried I'll find him as frozen as everything around him. He's never painted or sculpted a thing, but he lives for art.'

Outside that world of statues, Paris was still very much alive. The streets were full of passersby who constantly changed direction, as if suddenly remembering something they had to do; the trees rustled even though there was no wind; not even the houses were still but shook with the passing of cars. And yet, as I approached rue des Cendres (named because of a brick factory that used to blanket the street in ash), there were fewer people, and everything turned gray, still, and empty. I passed a dead beggar and a sleeping horse. Mattioli's house, at the end of the street, was like something from a dream, the kind of house you only ever see from the outside because, the moment you knock, you startle awake.

I found a window at street level and stretched out on the cobblestones. Through the dirty glass, I could see into Mattioli's studio. His tools were on the floor; there was a folding screen at the back. Sketches of the model multiplied her figure countless times. The sculptor was working on a block of marble he had already transformed into the shadow of a woman.

Clarissa was off to one side: naked, white, perfect – more perfect even than the distant copy her father had made. She was gripping a gold helmet and a lance that rested on the floor beside her. She sat so still that, in contrast, the other Clarissa, the one born out of marble, seemed to be alive.

A Blank Page

Von Knepper was leaning over a delicate mechanism that resembled a musical instrument: glass pegs tightened very fine strings that would make a sound at the slightest touch.

'We need to find another way to make automatons talk. The human vocal system is extremely difficult to control. The slightest imperfection and the melody of the inanimate starts to play. One day I'll resort to magic. I once read that Hermes Trismegistus could make a statue so perfect that life was inevitable.'

'A statue that comes to life must also then die.'

'Maybe the Egyptian sorcerers watched theirs weaken and expire, and abandoned the method forever. Who knows, maybe their creatures reverted to statues, only this time they were abominable, or maybe they shattered into piles of marble shards.'

I picked up a hand that was on the table and tested it. The bones were made of black wood and the joints of gold.

'I found Clarissa,' I said nonchalantly.

Von Knepper's hands leaped to my neck and he repeated his daughter's name, as if it were a threat. He squeezed my throat with professional rigor. I fought in vain for the air that would allow me to speak. In the midst of our struggle, we fell on the table. The tiny harp – future throat – fell to the floor, making a strange sound, like an animal cry. Heeding this plea, Von Knepper released me. I backed into a corner of the room.

'I don't have her, but I know where she is. I saw her myself. I'll take her somewhere safe today.'

'And do you think I'm going to just wait here, doing nothing, while you. . .?'

'You won't be doing nothing. I have a job for you.'

I pulled a ball of paper from my pocket. The documents that change a country's history, the secrets that send some to the throne and others to the gallows, aren't safely tucked in folders and covered in wax seals. They're wrinkled sheets of paper, dampened by the rain, that some insignificant person carries deep in his pocket, with coins, a penknife, and a bit of bread.

'This is the text the bishop is to write. Three envoys from Rome will be meeting with him the day after tomorrow.'

'Yes, I know about that meeting. I was told to make the final adjustments.'

'Those adjustments are written here.'

He read the page.

'You're crazy. If the bishop writes this, his skull will become an inkwell and my blood the ink.'

'I understand the danger, but there's no other way for you to see your daughter again.'

Disheartened, Von Knepper read the message over and over. It may not have been the thought of Clarissa that changed his mind, but the message itself: after all, it was the truth.

'Once the new text has been written, you won't able to come back here. At least not while Mazy remains in power.'

'I have somewhere to hide. I've spent my life living under aliases, in houses rented for three months at a time. What about my daughter?'

I handed him a blank page.

'She's here.'

He turned the sheet over and, seeing it was blank as well, threw it in my face. I handed it back.

'It's invisible ink. The message will appear in a little more than forty hours without you doing anything. Forget about using sulfur, alcohol, saltpeter, or any other thing you might think of; all you'll find then is an illegible smudge. Keep your promise and the secret will be revealed.'

When I left Von Knepper's, I walked to the Seine and quietly asked at a bookstore for *The Bishop's Message*.

'Sold out,' the bookseller said. It was hard to know if he was telling the truth or was afraid I was an inspector.

Voltaire's first message was already in print, and being passed from hand to hand all over the city. His second would soon be engraved on an iron plate, and fill the bishop's memory with forty-two words.

Hammer and Chisel

There were two statues in Mattioli's studio. One had Clarissa's features; the other was covered by a gray cloth. The sculptor had collapsed into a chair, and his threadbare shirt only exaggerated the defeat in his posture. Kolm was holding the hammer and chisel at shoulder height on the statue and tapping. Shards and dust were falling from the marble.

'Where is she?'

'I hired her, but she left without a word.'

Kolm tapped again, only harder this time. He had started at the edge of the block, but was now moving toward the already well-defined face.

197

'I've never carved a head like this one. The girl's gone, and all I have of her is what you see there.'

Kolm seemed to have forgotten his purpose was to threaten, and had become enthused by the tools. He frightened me a little, so I decided to take advantage of that:

'They say every block of marble has a particular spot on which the life of the stone depends. Once you hit it, the marble will crack. How long until my friend finds that spot?'

Kolm aimed the next blow at the statue's invisible heart. I jumped, sure the execution would be final this time. Mattioli didn't bat an eyelid. He spoke with the wisdom of someone who has won or lost everything:

'I've had dozens of models, but none of them was still enough. Those hands that would rise up to brush away a fly; those eyes that would seek who knows what outside the window. Boredom, nerves, exhaustion. They thought they were being still, but I saw the silent dance: first the foot, then the elbow, and, when their own nakedness bothered them, the rapid breath or syncopated heartbeat. But then I found her, down in the basement, among the others at the Académie. My colleagues – those good for nothings – didn't even see her because they don't know how to look. I've been searching for her for years; I even wrote a book exalting her absence. And then suddenly there she was.'

We had searched for Clarissa as well, all through the house, even the basement and the attic. Getting around was no easy task; the hallways were blocked not only by unfinished sculptures and paintings, but also the instruments Mattioli had used to pursue his ideal of stillness. As the search wore on, the artist began to explain the nature of his collection with a certain amount of pride. There were music boxes that caused momentary immobility, a seat fitted with metal brackets and belts, and bottles of narcotic drugs (which almost forced us to abandon the hunt because of the toxic cloud that filled the attic). In a corner we found a suit of armor made of iron bands that left sections of the victim bare. Bronze spikes in the most painful places ensured the model would sit still.

There was only one place left to look. I walked toward the second statue and pulled off the gray cloth. Kolm had glanced there earlier, but had mistaken her for a real statue. Clarissa was posed like before, only minus the lance and gold helmet. I kissed her icy lips and, in doing so, grew angry that her naked body was in full view. Behind the folding screen, in among easels and rolled up canvases, was some clothing that might have been hers. I dressed her in silence. Clarissa didn't seem to know where she was when she awoke, and I waited for her memory to make sense of the room.

She walked over to the work in progress and ran her fingers over the statue's face.

'Did I do alright, Mattioli?'

'No one has ever done better. But now it will never be finished.'

'Then it will be just like me. I'm not finished either.'

Not finding any warm clothes, I put my cloak around Clarissa and we left Mattioli's house. At some point, Kolm disappeared without a word. He might have tried to say good-bye, but I only had eyes for Clarissa. A coach took us to the Académie des Beaux-Artes, but we didn't go in right away in case Mattioli had decided to follow us.

I knocked repeatedly until the door was finally opened. The boy painter had been asleep, and stared at me blankly.

'Arsit, this is the friend I told you about. You need to look after her until her father, M. Laghi, comes to get her.'

I handed him the amount we had agreed on that afternoon. It would have been easy to cheat Arsit; he seemed completely unaware of the value of money, but I felt sorry for the boy painter.

'I'll use this opportunity to talk to her about art. I'll tell her the story behind every statue, and I won't even charge for it.'

Clarissa was awake now.

'Why did you bring me here?'

'You need to stay here until your father arrives. The abbot's men will be looking for you both.'

'Why? What has my father done?'

'Nothing yet, but it won't be long.'

'At one time I thought you'd rescue me from my father and help me escape. Instead, here you are turning me over to him. You call that love?'

Around us the crowd of statues seemed to grow larger and cast a disapproving murmur in my direction. Fingers and swords pointed at me. Arsit furrowed his brow in silence, as if he had to show a certain amount of indignation toward me, and yet didn't want to get too involved – as annoyed as any child by incomprehensible adult problems.

Clarissa disappeared among the statues, without a word, as if she knew her way, as if she were returning to her birthplace.

Arsit looked at me with wide eyes, slightly overwhelmed by the sense of responsibility. He counted the money – or pretended to count it – and then, as if accepting his position as king of that underground world, ordered me to leave with a wave of his hand.

The Locked Door

The one hundred copies Hesdin had printed were soon sold out among the Pont Neuf booksellers, where a whole community of obsessive readers went in search of forbidden words. Most of them were spies, paid by the Church or the police to obtain texts and study them. Even innocent readers wanted to join their ranks as this assured them unrestricted access to books, and the money to buy them. In exchange, they simply had to add a title to the index every now and then. There was no higher prestige than the sparkle of the flames; they only increased the mystery surrounding a book, and its price.

Ever since the *Encyclopédie* appeared, the number of these

undercover agents had grown. They were the first to leap on every new release and vie for the copies. One informant didn't know another: each believed he was the only spy in a world of innocents. There were readers trained in Athanasius Kircher's cryptography who could decipher any code; others interpreted the pages in terms of political allegory; and the most keenly intelligent, prepared to arrive at innocence through the complexities of intellect, were charged with the literal meaning. Through one method or another, every interpreter found a hidden truth.

The Jesuits had come to dominate the literal interpretation, which was actually the most difficult. Believing that an attack on the Dominicans might improve their position, they disseminated their own version of *The Bishop's Message*. At the time, I had no idea of the journey that story had taken, and believed it had been swallowed up, like so many other books printed in Paris every day. Often they would shine while a conversation or a dinner lasted, and then disappear without any need for bonfires.

I walked past the Auberge du Poisson, afraid to go in until I was sure no one was waiting for me. If Von Knepper had kept his word, the other message, that brief confession, would already be engraved on a metal plate and have taken

over the automaton's memory. I took a stroll and soon discovered one of the abbot's guards. Tired of the wait, he was
pretending to be blind, stretching his long, yellow fingers
out to passersby who were trying to avoid him. He had
begun to take his disguise so seriously that he was whis-
pering who knows what threats into the ears of pedestri-
ans, reaching out for them with his cane, its sharpened tip
encouraging charity. He was a failure as a spy but a success
as a beggar, and the hours of waiting had filled his pockets.
I walked away with my eyes closed, like a child hoping not
to be seen. I wandered the city for the rest of the day, not
knowing where to spend the night that was coming, the
night that had arrived, the night that was ending.

Very early the next morning, almost unintentionally,
my footsteps led me to L'école de Medécine. Perhaps
Kolm would still be there, testing his machine. The iron
gate was open. When I reached the long, empty corridor,
I could hear the sound of keys in the distance. I was so
afraid of that noise, I had to convince myself the sense of
danger was only in my imagination.

The room where Kolm was searching for the perfect machine was locked, but there would be no shortage of keys to unlock it. Signac, accompanied by the

blind pretender, was suddenly beside me. The keeper of the keys held a lamp over my head, while his colleague brought the sharpened tip of his cane to my throat.

'All our lives, we open and close doors, without realizing the consequences,' Signac said. 'It's like in the fairy-tales: one door leads to the treasure and the other to the dragon's den.'

Signac handed me a key. I knew something terrible was going to happen the moment I opened the door. I recalled the story of the Syracusans: perhaps I had come to the room where an executioner was waiting for me.

The key turned easily in the lock. It took some effort to push the door open, however, as the end of a rope was lodged between it and the frame. The door finally gave way and the rope was released.

I heard the whisper of the blade and then the impact. I don't know whether Kolm had ever managed to test his machine on a cadaver, but it worked perfectly that time. The blade slid down the greased rails and cut cleanly. The head fell on the wooden floor and rolled to my feet. Kolm's eyes were still open.

Signac lifted the lamp, and I could see the machine looked exactly like the illustration of the Halifax gibbet.

Kolm's body was tied to a long table. His hair and the collar of his shirt had been cut to facilitate the blade's work. I was still holding the key that had made me the executioner's executioner.

'Do you know what Kolm said when I explained my plan?' Signac asked with a push, forcing me to walk down the corridor. 'Now anyone can be an executioner.'

I heaved a sigh of relief at leaving that blood-stained room. The blind pretender walked ahead. The keeper of the keys came behind, locking doors as he passed.

Silas Darel

We crossed the central patio with its thorny plants and blue leaves used for calligraphic pursuits. In the middle of the courtyard were two deep ponds made of black marble. There were sturgeon, squid, and a fish that glowed in the deep: all of them used to make ink. In no hurry, the keeper of the keys and the blind pretender led me across patios and up stairs.

We finally came to the calligraphy hall. Tomes as big as coffins stood on the bookcase. An astonishing collection of quills and inks filled cabinets and shelves. The smell of the inks mingled with the stuffy air. In among bottles stacked in the shape of a tower, a star, a cross, I saw a human skull that was used as an inkwell and quills so enormous it was hard to imagine what bird they had been plucked from. The two guards who had brought me moved away, leaving me apparently free. Such implements could only have belonged to Silas Darel. I began to look all around me, in search of the great calligrapher, when I saw a small office. It was down a few stairs; I had to duck my head to enter.

Darel was working and didn't look up. His hands were so white and fine it was as if a sudden movement might break them; his long nails looked like slivers of marble. He was concentrating on every stroke, writing slowly and forcefully, giving the words a definitive quality. This contrasted with the faint shadow of his hand on the paper, and was itself another form of writing that seemed to say: for every word that remains, countless others disappear.

The calligrapher's silence was like a glass wall around him. I've heard that focus is a form of prayer; if that's the case, this man was most certainly praying. The light coming in through a small window fell across a Venetian inkwell filled with blood.

I was trying to see what Darel was writing, looking for my name among the red words, when the answer came from behind me.

'He's writing our history,' said the abbot, who had come in quietly. 'But he's not bound by the usual rule of waiting until things have happened. He's finished with the past, and is now busy with the future. Our enemies have the *Encyclopédie* and the will to clarify all things; we have calligraphy and a duty to mystify the world.'

The sound of pealing bells seemed to reach us from far away. The abbot unrolled a piece of paper before me.

'I want you to write your confession. Who sent you and why. Every word must be true. Our master calligrapher doesn't hear but only sees, and can recognize the hesitation of a lie in handwriting. If that happens, he will plunge his quill into your neck before you know it. I'm sorry I won't be here to watch the exam, but the envoys from Rome are waiting.'

A small inkwell was set in front of me and a quill placed in my hand. The abbot hurried to the door, accompanied by the keeper of the keys. The other guard had disappeared. Darel opened a drawer and pulled out a sharpened quill, the tip so pointed it would tear the paper at the slightest touch.

I slowly wrote the truth, wondering whose blood was now my ink. I tried to delay putting the name Voltaire on paper. Darel, who didn't read the words, but only the handwriting, must have noticed something because he attacked me with his quill, wounding me on the face. The pain forced me to stop. I pulled out a handkerchief and, when I brought it to my cheek, a strange symbol was imprinted on it.

I didn't want him to hurt me again. What was so absolutely true that Darel would refrain from attacking me? I recalled how we used to repeat his name, in secret, in the cloisters at Vidors' School. I had finally seen the legend, and the legend was going to kill me. Slowly, as slowly as the automaton, I wrote the text the bishop was writing at the very same time before the eyes of Rome:

Do not look for the bishop in these hands...

Hieroglyphic

The envoys from Rome had read the Jesuit interpretation of *The Bishop's Message* and came prepared to understand: they arrived at the palace with an escort of twenty-five men. When the signal came, when Von Knepper's creature wrote the forty-two words dreamed up in Ferney, there was no need to ask for an explanation:

> *Do not look for the bishop in these hands.*
> *I am in an unmarked grave,*
> *With no purple or scepter*

Because an impostor has taken my place.
The abbot has written my words until now.
This time, however, I speak for myself.

I heard a commotion in the distance and, through the window, saw monks fleeing from the Roman soldiers. Doors that were being ripped opened and slammed shut in the distance called out to Signac, the keeper of the keys. My guard understood his duty lay elsewhere, and was faithful to the end.

Darel paid no attention to what was going on outside, but focused solely on the task he had been given. I admired his infinite concentration: not once did he turn his head to look out the window. He was indifferent to it all, and simply wrote.

Down there, in the geometric garden, the keeper of the keys, in bloodied clothes, obliterated all symmetry. Staggering, he battled four men whose daggers had already wounded him. He mortally injured one, but lost his weapon in the thrust and very nearly his hand. Just when it seemed he had lost, he pulled out two colossal keys, destined for who knows what unimaginable doors. True to their purpose, they opened two skulls. The only foe left standing leaped on the giant, who tripped over one of the wounded and fell into the black pond.

Signac tried to remove the weight that was pulling him down, but the keys never ended: once he had unclipped the keys to the main doors, there were still those to the cellar, not to mention the great doors onto the garden, the chapel, the secret chambers, the museum, the catacombs, the calligraphy hall, Darel's office. It may have been a gust of wind that blew from one end of the palace to the other, but the moment Signac hit bottom, I heard distant doors slam in what sounded like a funeral salute. A school of disconcerted sturgeon swam in circles above the fallen giant.

Darel was prepared to discover my lie but, inspired as it was by the truth, never saw the final stroke coming: my quill leaped from the page and plunged into his neck. I stood prepared for his response, but he never even looked at me. Darel knew how to recognize the stroke of a pen; he knew this was the last word. He covered his wound with a white hand that was soon red, and walked to his desk. With a tremor that would surely have mortified him, he drew the same symbol he had earlier drawn with a steady hand on my face.

214

In the years that followed, every time I looked in a mirror, I envied the hand that had written that symbol. At the time it seemed to have no meaning. Whenever I suffered from insomnia, I would copy it over and over, until I was sure I was about to solve the mystery, but then I would fall asleep.

Only years later, here in this new land, did I discover its meaning in an old newspaper, when the truth about Egyptian hieroglyphics came to light: it was the hieroglyph for the god Thot, who invented writing. But how could Darel have known that? It was then I remembered the story I'd heard at Vidors' School: the story of an ancient tradition of scribes that had continued uninterrupted, across continents and through catastrophes.

Sometimes, when I look at my face by the light of the moon in a small, broken mirror that hangs on my wall, I tell myself that Darel marked me so I would know something grand and secret ended with me.

Inventory

On a corner of my desk is all the work I have to do: write up agreements for immediate signature, detail expenses from the last two months, prepare a clean copy of two court rulings. Any documents that put the security of the state at risk are entrusted to someone else. If they see me as being so different, and therefore suspicious, it's not because they're thinking of France, but that enormous and exotic realm: the past.

After the events at Arnim Palace, I returned to Ferney, where I worked as calligrapher for seventeen years. I never did set up my workshop with quills and inks, choosing a safer and more idle life instead. In the mornings

I attended to Voltaire's correspondence and sometimes his books; in the afternoons I dealt with his commercial paperwork and drafted documents. It was a peaceful job, and I would have liked it to last forever.

Many years later, when Voltaire announced he was going to Paris, I felt there was nothing left for me at Ferney. Everyone else agreed; they all carried out every act – cleaning a vase, preparing a meal, pruning the yellow rosebushes – with the care and indifference particular to those who know they are doing it for the very last time.

Those of us who accompanied Voltaire's carriage as it left did so in silence. We were supposed to be celebrating, but it felt more like a funeral cortège. The mood turned out to be appropriate: Paris awaited Voltaire to shower him with every imaginable honor, to subject him to a stream of visitors at Mme Villette's hotel, to exhaust him to death, and then deny him burial.

Voltaire's heart arrived at Château Ferney two months after his death. The only grave they found for him was on the outskirts of the city, in Sellières, where his nephew was abbot. Before his body was buried, the doctor removed his heart. He acted as if it were an impromptu operation, but it was obvious to those in attendance that the decision had been made much earlier: on a night when urgency and chaos reigned, he had brought several jars of salt, and a blue liquid that irritated the eyes. I don't know who might have fought over the heart, or who sent it to Ferney; it was delivered by a Polish messenger who spoke not a word of French and stayed no more than a minute.

In the confusion that now governed the house, the heart was put in the study, with all of the eccentricities distinguished travelers had brought from distant lands over the years. No one had gone in there since Voltaire's death, and the pieces were now covered in cobwebs and dust. The master of the house was gone, and the house itself seemed to sicken and die. The heart lay forgotten among rocks that shone in the dark, sea creatures, and unicorn bones.

I was assigned to take inventory. As soon as I noted things down they would disappear, and before long almost none of the eccentricities were left. It was common to see the servants' children out in the garden playing with a whale jawbone, a polar bear hide, or a martyr's mummified hand.

At first I tried to maintain a certain sense of order, but in the end I joined the looters and hid the heart among my things. So no one would notice its absence, I put the embalmed heart of a sixteenth century Venetian countess in its place – a gift from Voltaire's friend, the marquis d'Argenson.

I finished the inventory one day before leaving. My handwriting was no longer what it was when I started: it was now serene and simple and made no attempt to dazzle. It was the writing of someone who knows that the words on the page hide both what's there and what's lost.

The Marble Head

Catherine the Great inherited the archives, and the secretaries and file clerks who were bound to those pages for life went with them. I didn't want that fate and returned to Paris, with Voltaire's heart among my belongings.

I worked in the mornings as a calligraphy expert at Siccard House (the second floor activities had been shut down) and spent my afternoons looking for Clarissa. There was no trace of her or her father anywhere in the city. To a certain extent, I've never abandoned the search: even here in this faraway port, whenever newcomers have passed through France, I find them to see if they've heard the name Von Knepper.

I only ever came across one witness, and that witness I lost. The night before I left, I was walking along the Seine when a bearded man in rags stepped out in front of me. I had seen him from afar on other occasions: he would stop passersby, show them something he carried in a bag, and let them go. But this time he startled me: for a moment I thought he was going to kill me so I drew my only weapon, the quill I had used to kill Silas Darel. Despite the beard and the darkness, I recognized Mattioli but he didn't seem to know who I was. Showing me the contents of a bag he could barely lift, he asked:

'Have you seen this woman?'

'No,' I replied, in barely a whisper.

'It's all over then,' the sculptor said, as if his last hope had died with me, there was no one left in the entire city to ask.

He climbed up onto the railing with a familiarity that obviated any sense of danger. Before securing the knot that tied the bag around his neck, he looked at the marble head one last time. I ran to stop him: I too wanted to kiss those icy lips. He didn't give me a chance. Mattioli embraced the head and jumped into the dark waters. The last image of Clarissa drowned with him.

Buenos Aires, December 1998 – July 2001